HER VAMPIRE PRINCE

DARK VINTAGE
BOOK 1

INES JOHNSON

THOSE JOHNSON GIRLS

All rights reserved. This copy is intended for the original purchaser of this book ONLY. No part of this book may be reproduced, scanned, or distributed in any printed or electronic form without prior written permission from the authors. Please do not participate in or encourage piracy of copyrighted materials in violation of the authors' rights. Purchase only authorized editions.

Published in the United States of America

Second Edition: June 2024

This book is a work of fiction. While reference might be made to actual historical events or existing locations, the names, characters, places and incidents are either the product of the authors' imaginations or are used fictitiously, and any resemblance to actual persons, living or dead, business establishments, events, or locales is entirely coincidental.

1

———

Hadrian

I see the invaders on the horizon. For the last ten hours, they have battered the safe house where I've holed up. They're an army of many where I am only one. If a breach were to happen it would be a massacre. Their sheer numbers would overwhelm me in an instant and I would be but dust.

Victory is in sight as the terrorists begin their retreat. Their bright orange armor grows dim as the pale moon rises. Their yellow arms slink slowly behind the vista as the dark of night falls.

I feel strong today. Strong and filled with a passion I haven't felt in many years. Rational thought flees my mind. I yank the door open and charge into the twilight. My bare feet slice into blades of grass. My bare ass cheeks clench at the chill in the air. I don't get far before I'm hit.

Right in the junk.

A cloud shifts and an errant sun ray warms my right testicle. To the everyday man, this would be a pleasant tingle. Might even give him a stiffy first thing in the morning.

It is not morning. Night has fallen.

I am not a man. I am a vampire.

And the sun just kicked me in the nuts.

I drop to my knees and cup my jewels. Cursing that fucking star in the sky.

2

____

Cari

I've scaled a volcano and could barely feel the heat. I've hiked the Arctic tundra hardly sensing the cold. I even tried that walk-on-glass thing. I didn't feel the glass pierce my bare feet. But damn was the cleanup of the tiny shards in my toes a whole lot of mess to deal with afterward.

But that's me these days. I walk around with my entire body pretty much numb. Cold, hot, sharp? They're all dull. So light rarely penetrates me.

I do what every child knows not to do. I look directly into the sun. It couldn't possibly cause any more damage.

But the sun has set. The bright rays sinking beneath the horizon. It can't hurt me. Nothing can.

I've been on over a dozen skydiving jumps in the months since my dad died. That's only half of the required number of jumps for a night jump license. Meaning technically I'm not qualified to be up here staring out of the open door of a plane after the sunset, preparing to jump. Luckily, the amount of money I have in the bank bests my lacking qualifications.

My trust fund money also gets the pilot to fly over my family's estate rather than the approved drop zone. I am by no means a spoiled brat. Neither of my siblings are either. Our father taught us the value of every dollar that was put into our accounts. My brother Arneis parlayed his inheritance into a career of community service. My sister Marechal turned her coin and her consideration toward science.

Me? Well, I'd only just turned twenty-one when my dad died. I was on the cusp of figuring out what I wanted to do with my life when it all turned upside down.

I tug at my safety harness, the only thing that gives me a sense of security these days. My equipment has already been checked and double-checked. They've outfitted me with a lighted altimeter so I'll know when to deploy the chute. I also receive a flashlight and a whistle. The weather is a go with not a storm cloud in sight.

Looking down, all is dark. The sight below me is a disappointment. I hoped my childhood memories would flood back to my mind and make my heart swell with nostalgia. But it isn't like walking the vineyard while atop my dad's shoulders. I can't see much of anything except dark clumps and rows.

Still, the adrenaline rushing through me at being in the air can't be beat. I feel. I *can* feel. In the air is the only time sensation visits me.

I revel in it. There are no decisions to make. No one I'll hurt. There is only the wind and the warmth. Why can't this feeling last forever?

But it can't. No matter how high I go the ground always comes at me.

I can buy another flight. I can take another dive into the abyss. But I can't buy more time in the free fall. My father's money can't give me any more time with him. All I want is to stretch out the last second when my dad was alive and still with me.

I know the numbness will return as soon as my feet touch land. The indecision. The lack of direction. The emptiness. The guilt. The shame.

I shouldn't be here in this plane. I shouldn't be here in the clouds. I should be in the ground with him. But I survived the crash without a scratch.

I stand now, strapped into a safety harness and prepare to jump out of a perfectly good airplane. I don't step out of the plane. I take a running leap. My swan dive might resemble a swan song. It's not, though. This won't be my last performance in the air.

I'll land on the ground. Not a scratch on me. Again.

And then I'll do it again. And probably again. I don't know what else to do.

I free-fall, finding something close to joy in the temporary sensations that wake up my body and brain. Maybe if I could make this last a few more minutes I could figure out what to do with my life.

Too late. My time is already up. The altimeter lights up, alerting me that it is time to deploy the chute.

I hesitate, my thumb lingering over the button. I know death isn't the answer. Just these few seconds that separate life from death. That's where I want to live.

I'll land and let the numbness take me tonight. Tomorrow I'll look for another adventure. One that lasts longer in that stretch between life and death. But first I have to survive this landing. Too bad my fingers are numb.

The air slapping me in the face tries to nudge me into action. Finally, I press the button to release the chute. There is the telltale whirring as the chute releases from my pack. Then the normal jerk followed by a tug as the fabric unfolds. That jerk of the harness signals to my body that the warm sensation is coming to a close; like an elevator announcing landing on the ground floor.

I feel the jerk of the harness that holds my parachute. Then it loosens. Wait? That's not supposed to happen.

The binds of the harness go slack and let me go. The last thing in this world that makes me feel safe has let me down. Now that the tension of the rope is gone I feel bereft, lost.

I'm truly going down. The chute flaps in the air above me. A white flag flailing in surrender.

This is it. This is actually it. I'm going to die.

No.

That can't be right.

I'm invincible. I survived a fatal car crash without a scratch. I've been on over a dozen jumps. I walked a freaking volcano in sandals. I swam with fucking sharks while on my damn period.

Skydiving is the only place I find any peace. No. This is not going to be taken from me. I'm not going out like this.

There's still the reserve parachute. I reach for the catch, but my fingers fumble. The ground is approaching so fast. Will I even have time to open the reserve?

My fingers find the release. The second chute shoots from my pack. There is no jerk of my harness. There is no plume spread over my head like a halo.

For the first time in a year, I feel fear. The second chute has failed. The fabric blows in the wind like a sinking kite. I am the string, dangling from the end. Only unlike a flyaway kite, the chute and I are falling fast to the earth.

This is it. This is the end. I'm going to die. No seatbelt, no harness, no nothing will save me.

Without the balance of the chute, I begin to tumble head over feet. The ropes tangle my limbs until I can't move. I am bound and headed for the ground.

I try to force my eyes shut. But the wind keeps my lids open. I don't want to see this. I don't want to witness another death, not even my own.

But I have no choice. My demise is fast approaching. I can almost make out the young buds on the vines. My blood will taint the crops. Marechal will be pissed that I ruined her hybrids. Arneis will be put out that my death will make the local news. It won't likely help either of my siblings; Marechal for business, Arneis for the polls.

Damn. Even in my death, I will hurt them.

Just before impact, I am granted one blessing. My eyes shut as I await the crash.

3

Hadrian

"Thank you for choosing Sorority Chicks Hauling Ass for your moving needs today, Mr. Serrano."

I take the clipboard from the chick-in-charge. Her demeanor does remind me of a chicken. Small blonde head with tail feathers drooping over her ass. I think those particular decorative feathers are called Daisy Dukes; short shorts that could double as a thong. Her breasts are large enough to make a succulent Sunday dinner.

I scrawl my name on the dotted line, remembering to write using English characters instead of the Roman ones I grew up with. Luckily, the name I go by in this day and age doesn't contain any of the letters that hadn't come into existence during the height of Rome.

"That vintage chair looks like something out of the Spanish Inquisition," she says.

So, the sorority chick's IQ is a few sizes bigger than her tits. The chair is straight out of the Inquisition; a souvenir from my time in those dungeons where I elicited confessions from sinners, and sometimes the innocent depending on my mood and what I'd eaten the prior day.

It was once known as a Chair of Torture. Its main feature was a set of spikes at the back. I was more fond of using the wrist ties to hold my victims still while I went about my business. I kept a gaping hole in the seat where other torturers would use hot coals. In my former line of work, I found that a strip of velvet, or a wet tongue, or a sculpted dildo got far more confessions. Orgasms loosened lips far more than singed and torn skin.

"Are you building a Red Room of Pain?"

I can see the chick's dark nipples staring back at me through the translucent shirt. I'm not interested. Not that her double G's aren't impressive. Another man would surely be impressed. Undoubtedly the one who hired her would. I'll point her in Gaius' direction, after I murder him for this latest stunt.

These chicks should have been done with the job of moving crates and boxes into my new home hours ago. But here it is after sunset and they are struggling to bring down the last object.

My patience at an end, I go over and tip the dolly forward. I don't need the wheeled device to lift the crate. I also don't need or want the sorority chicks to see my strength. I especially don't need any more tits hardening in my direction. Unfortunately, I do not get my wish.

I get the box down easily enough. But the crate door slides open revealing its contents. There is a chorus of feminine gasps that remind me of the chirps of chicks hungry for seed.

Inside the confines of the wooden box is another wooden frame. At one end of the frame is a roller where hands would be bound. A fixed bar sits at the other end where legs would be fastened. The apparatus was used to stretch the body until its victim spilled the truth. Or had all their bones broken. Whichever came first.

Back in my time, a rack would elicit nothing but shrieks of terror. That is until I got my victims rolling on it. Then the mind would bend as I took them through the paces of sweet agony and bitter pleasure. My hands knew exactly what buttons to press to give toe-curling pleasure as well as back-cracking convulsions.

"Can Mr. Grey see me now?" says one sorority chick. Her question is followed by wanton giggles from the rest of her brood.

These women do not know what they're asking for. In this new world, spending a night with a Dom is a bucket list item for most. They do not know who they're dealing with. I was a libertine before de Sade. I was a rake before Casanova. I had the hip swivel down before that jailhouse rocking singer in a jumpsuit. But unlike all those men, my submissives never left my dungeon.

Save one.

And she is the reason all of these toys are going into the cellar below my new home and not put to use in some brightly colored day room.

"I've left a tip," I say as I usher the sorority chicks out of the door.

"I bet I could earn a larger one," says the head chick.

There is a Pear of Anguish tucked into the rack. With a twist of the knob, the petals of the device expand in the mouth to cut off the voice and the air passages. The Pear is the precursor to the modern day ball gag. I'd threaten this woman with it but I'm sure it would only get her feathers wet.

Instead of using a device, I stare into the chick's eyes. It doesn't take much more than a nudge to push the suggestion in her mind that I remind her of her chemistry professor, the one whose shriveled cock she got down on her knees and sucked. Then he still gave her a D in the course. The memory gets her in her truck and she hauls her ass off my property and into the night.

I am alone with my solitude at last. I lock the door to the cellar, shutting off that part of me, and step out into the night. The ground is still warm from the setting sun. I can almost feel the heat as I take a walk across my family's new enterprise and once again leave my old life behind.

The devices are a reminder, not that I could ever forget. Domitia loved being strapped into the Chair of Torture with her wrists bound and her legs spread wide. I'd pull orgasm after orgasm from her until she begged me to yank out one more. I'd stretch her body over the rack and fuck her until she passed out. Pain turned to pleasure until we fell into oblivion. But that life is over.

The grapes of our new vineyard are just starting to bud. Winter cold has given way to spring delights. The vines struggle a bit as they've been taken out of their native soil of Italy and transplanted in this foreign land. This is exactly how my second life with her began.

Domitia compelled me to follow her the last night of my human life. Her fangs on my neck were more exquisite than any orgasm. A vampire's bite is akin to ecstasy, if done right. And Domitia performed expertly.

I was so enraptured with her that I didn't begrudge the fact that I was dying. I was certain she loved me when she cut open the flesh at her heart to rejuvenate me. She fed me her blood and brought me back to life; a life of darkness and pain when she slipped through my fingers, out the door, and into the light of the sun.

I haven't touched a woman in nearly two hundred years. Domitia had been my last. She would be my only. I owed her that much since I couldn't save her.

Outside the moon has taken command in the sky. Stars twinkle. Clouds move with no hurry. Except one.

That particular cloud moves fast as a storm

readying to break through and pelt the ground with a downpour. But there is no rain in the forecast. The cloud moves south instead of to the east or west. It is coming straight at me. And it has legs. Because it is a woman falling from the sky. And she is falling fast.

4

———

Cari

I started doing adrenaline adventures shortly after we buried my father. At first, the trips were low-risk enough. In fact, the experiences were therapy.

I wouldn't get behind the wheel of a car for weeks after the crash. A therapist suggested exposure therapy. For my first session, I went on a race track and had a professional race car driver take me around the circular track. By the time he pulled back into the pit, I was squirming in my seat and clutching at the seatbelt.

I returned later and had the hot race car driver

drive me around the track at top speed. It was the speed that revved my engines. The knowledge that we could crash at any time--that was what made me come back to life. The moment he pressed the brake, I started to cool. By the time he cut the engine and loosened his seatbelt to try to make out, I was cold. I bought a Miata the next day.

Unfortunately, speed soon lost my interest. There is only so fast a car could go. Height became my new drug of choice. But even skydiving had begun losing that initial thrill. Once I land I go numb quicker and quicker.

Except now.

After my parachute and my spare fail, I close my eyes and await impact. Hitting the ground isn't as painful as I'd thought it would be. In fact, it feels only as if I've been tossed up in the air and caught. Caught by a strong set of arms.

Arms I wouldn't mind snuggling into. Arms I wouldn't mind hitting the brakes for. Arms that make me feel I'm still falling from the sky, but at the same time safe, secure, and warm.

I chance to open my eyes only to find I am being cradled in the arms of the most beautiful man I've ever seen. The feel of his hands wrapped around me keeps my blood hot. Even though we aren't skin to skin, goosebumps are everywhere.

My fingertips feel singed inside my protective gloves. My nipples are tight points that could've cut through the layers. Is that his hand on my ass? Between my thighs, my core is hot even in the cool air of the night.

Even if it is his hand and not the harness on my ass there is nothing I can do. I am bound in my harness and the cords of the defunct chute. Yet somehow, I feel safe, content, and totally at peace at this moment of my demise.

Death has me in his clutches and there is nothing I can do about it. My adrenaline spikes higher. But there is no fear.

Fuck, I am truly messed up in the head.

"Am I dead?" I ask.

Death doesn't answer. His gaze is locked on mine. But I can see his pupils are dilated and roving over my features. I feel as if a dangerous predator has me over a boiling pot of water. Or rather, is about to stretch me over a raging fire. And for some reason, I don't seem to mind.

The way he's looking at me, I'm ready to bare my soul to his light eyes. His hair is the color of midnight and falls just above his shoulders in gentle waves. He has one of those patrician noses of a Roman sculpture, but it looks as though his nose has been broken a few times. The imperfection just makes him look all the more perfect. If this is what the Grim Reaper looks like I bet more women would be jumping out of airplanes.

Realizing that I'm in the Grim Reaper's clutches makes me realize another thing. There's someone else I want more than the one who holds me in his arms. "Will you take me to see my father?"

"Where's your father?"

His voice is like syrup on honey mixed in sweet wine. I want to shiver, but my body doesn't want to move a muscle inside his embrace.

"Wait?" I ask, the fear creeping back into me. "Is this heaven or hell?"

Again, he doesn't answer. There's a quirk at the corner of his mouth. It could be considered a grin, but it's there and gone in an instant.

"I suppose with what I did I probably ended up in hell," I say. "But this looks like a vineyard."

"It is a vineyard."

"Are you the devil?"

His lips break wide. I get a flash of teeth, white, gleaming, sharp. "I have been called that in the past. This is the Serrano vineyard."

"Serrano? The Serranos bought the old Palmezzo Vineyard."

"We did," he nods.

"It's a couple of miles over from my family's vineyard."

"Your family?"

"The Durands. I'm Carignan Durand."

"Hello, Carignan Durand. I'm Hadrian Serrano."

"Hadrian, that's nice." I smile as I use his first name and not his last.

He doesn't look old enough to be a Mr. Serrano. I wonder if it's his father that bought the vineyard. He did say family.

We stand there in silence for a moment. The crickets chirp, singing their mating call as they search for companionship for the night. A coyote howls at the moon in search of a booty call. An owl hoots into the wind, calling for some action of its own. All sounds of life and not what one would expect to hear in Hell.

"So, I'm not dead?" I ask.

5

____

Hadrian

I have a special talent. I can always identify someone who grew up on or worked for a vineyard. Even before I was turned. The smell of the vines seeps into their very pores. It was a different smell than a drunk's or wine enthusiast's smell. Those people only made contact with the berries. The others, the children of the vineyard, they had the sweet smell of berries, the tart taste of the vine, the pungent smell of the earth in their skin beneath their nails.

So she isn't a fallen angel. She is a human and

one who has grown up or worked around here by the smell of her.

She's slight. About fifty kilos or so. Her limbs are long and slender, like a gazelle. Her ass is a handful. I only know because that's how she lands.

I had to jump into the air to catch her. I know wine better than physics, but I do know enough to know that at the speed she was falling her bones would've broken if she'd landed in my arms from a fall that high. Her eyes were closed on the fall and so she didn't see that she was still in the air when I caught her.

Her shoulders are cradled inside my right forearm. Her ass right in the palm of my left hand. I fight the urge to squeeze, to test the plumpness of her flesh. Then I am surprised at my impulse. I've never groped anyone besides Domitia.

The fallen gazelle opens her eyes and I take in a breath. I see her perfectly in the dark; flushed pink cheeks, pert nose, and eyes a hazy color of cinnamon that reminds me of Chianti.

Her brows squish together as she tries to get a good look at me in the pale moonlight.

"So, I'm not dead?"

I don't answer her. I can't. My gaze is fastened on

her lips. The bright, vibrant, pulsing red line where there is a split at the center.

The smell of her warm blood curls up into the space between us. It is a sweetness I haven't smelled in a long time. Adrenaline mixed with blood. Sweet blood.

It is an aphrodisiac to vampires. It was my drug of choice during the Inquisition. I'd bind my victims with rope. Toying with them, torturing them, keeping them on that tightrope between pain and pleasure until their blood was the perfect blend for my tastes. But never have I smelled anything like this. Sweet blood from a child of the vines.

She thinks she is dead. Makes sense. She fell from the sky. And now she's in the clutches of a predator, one who hasn't had a drink from the veins in a very, very long time.

I'm hungry. Not just in my veins. A tendril of something is stretching up inside of me, awaking after a long slumber. I'm not sure what it is? But I have felt it before.

I have a new possession in my hands. I want to hold on to it. I want to protect it. I want to own it. More than likely, I'm just hungry.

"I can't believe I'm still alive," Carignan says.

She squirms in my arms. Reflexively my hands

tighten on the delicious bundle. I don't need to hold her so tight. She couldn't get away if I set her down. She is bound in ropes. They crisscross her chest, her torso, and her long legs. A bondage present delivered from the heavens to a sadist.

My throat waters. My pants tighten. I nearly drop her at the unfamiliar sensations. My dick hasn't gotten hard in a century. No, not even in wet dreams.

The only person I dream of is Domitia. Anytime she appears in my dreams there is no pleasure. Only pain in her eyes when I fail to save her.

"Did I hurt you?" Carignan asks.

I want to laugh, to eat, and possibly fuck, all at the same time. Instead, I can only gape. She thought she'd hurt me? My life has been nothing but pain. This tiny human can't even prick my skin much less harm me.

"God, I couldn't live with myself if I hurt another living soul."

Well, she is safe there. Technically, I am alive. There is a debate about whether or not I still have my soul.

"I'm fine," I say, needing to assure her for some reason. "I'm not the one who fell from the sky."

"My chute malfunctioned. And then my spare as

well. All the odds are against that happening, you know. I should be dead."

My fingers tighten around her. The hell is death taking anything else from me.

Not that she is mine.

So why am I not putting her down?

She gazes up at me; lost and vulnerable. This time I feel a definite twitch in my loins.

My fangs stab at my gums. I am suddenly thirsty. Even though I raided our stash of bagged blood earlier.

"You're trapped," I say.

Carignan looks down, noticing the harness and the ropes twining her arms and legs. She doesn't fight her captivity. Her body relaxes as though she's safe.

She is not.

"You're bleeding," I say. "I'm taking you inside."

The real question is will I allow her back out.

6

_____

Cari

Would this be the next rush I'd chase? Getting kidnapped by hot men who prowl vineyards in the night waiting for crazy chicks to fall from the sky? If so, it's not the worst way to spend a Friday night.

He's carrying me through the vineyards. I should tell him that I can walk. I'm not hurt. Once again, not a scratch on me as death ignores my knocking.

But I don't tell Hadrian that. I don't ask to be put down. Because since I've been in his arms I haven't stopped feeling.

Sensations are running all over my body, even

though I'm still strapped into the harness and the cords of the defunct parachute crisscross my arms and legs. So I keep quiet as he holds me close and walks towards the grand house that sits at the entrance to the vineyard.

"Tell me," Hadrian says. "Why would a human being jump out of a perfectly good airplane?"

I almost open my mouth and tell him the truth. That it is the only way I can feel anything. But I don't want him to think I am crazy... Crazier.

"I wanted to see the vineyard at night from up high."

It was a crazy idea to begin with. To try and recapture what it was like when I was a girl and my dad would lift me onto his shoulders and walk through our vineyard. But I'm full of nothing but crazy ideas these days.

Hadrian walks into an opened back door. The room is not a foyer. It's not a den. It's a bedroom. When he turns on the light, I get the sense it's *his* bedroom.

There are no pictures on the walls. In fact, the room is pretty sparse. There's only an oakwood chest next to a walk-in closet. There are no curtains, just blackout blinds that don't let in a hint of the moonlight we just stepped out of. The main feature in the room is a queen-sized bed fit for a king with a blood-red comforter and black silk pillows. The bed is made, I note.

"There are ladders," he says. "There are rooftops."

I stare at him in confusion. We are face to face since he still hasn't put me down. I know that when he finally does he'll have at least a foot on me. I hope that moment is far in the future. I like the air up here.

"To see the vineyard from up high," he says.

Oh. Right. We're back on my crazy.

Hadrian sits me down on his massive bed. My breath catches and my lips part as he crowds over me. His gaze slips to my lips and I see his nostrils flare.

Does he want to kiss me?

He could kiss me.

He could do anything he wants to me in my current predicament, bound as I am.

There is a tearing sound. At first, I think it's my breasts popping out of my shirt because my nipples are hard enough to cut through glass. But it's not my drill bits. He's breaking the ropes from the chute with his bare hands.

One by one they snap. That should not be possible. But neither should his game-winning catch of my body, either.

I gaze into his eyes. I can see them clearly now. They are the pale green of a white grape, the most common variety. But his are the seedless kind. I can't see his pupils now that we are in artificial light. Looking into his fathomless depths I feel like I'm falling.

"I think I might be invincible," I say.

I don't mean to say that. I've never told anyone my suspicions of being unbreakable.

Hadrian pulls the straps on my shoulders free. But he holds me in place with his gaze. My body is free, but I feel pinned. His fingertips brushing down my forearms are my new harness and I've never felt more secure.

"I should have died from that fall," I say.

"True."

"But here I am."

"You assume you're not in danger with me?"

I notice the accent now. Most of his responses have been monosyllabic. The cultured sound of his full sentence of words roll over me like honey.

I know I am in danger from that tilt of his lips. From the sparkle in his clear, green eyes. It's hypnotic.

"You make me feel warm," I admit.

OMG. How do I turn this thing called my mouth off? It just keeps going. Telling this stranger all of my secrets.

"I jumped out of that perfectly good airplane to feel warm," I say.

"I'm given to believe it's cold up there in the sky," Hadrian says. "Though I've never stepped out for a walk there, myself."

I can't place his accent. Not quite Spanish. He doesn't roll his R's. Italian, maybe? He has that rumble in the back of his throat with consonants. Definitely somewhere in Europe.

"Why are you cold?" he asks.

"My dad died," I say. "In a car accident. I was with him in the passenger seat. I survived without a single scratch. But now I'm numb. The only time I feel anything is when my life is in danger. So I've been doing adrenaline adventures. It makes me feel alive, warm. And then, when the danger is over, it all goes away."

There is no judgment in his eyes. He simply listens like he has all the time in the world. I like the way his gaze holds mine. For the first time in a year, it's as though someone actually hears me.

"Do you feel cold now?" he asks.

"No. I don't. I still feel warm. In my hands. My toes. My chest. In my..."

I bite my tongue. There is no way I'm gonna tell him that I am warm between my thighs. Hadrian smiles as though he knows where my mind just went.

"I feel warm everywhere," I settle on. "Why is that?"

"Perhaps your life is still in danger," he says.

"You won't hurt me."

His gaze slips then. I feel like he's cut me loose. I blink rapidly a few times, trying to catch my bearings as the world comes back into focus. He is still all I see.

His green gaze is on my lips. His hand reaches towards me. He presses his thumb across my lip.

Quick as a snake after an apple, my tongue strikes out. I meet the salt of his flesh but also taste the metallic tint of my blood on my lip.

7

____

Hadrian

I've met my fair share of masochists over the
centuries. Most masochists, and sadists for that
matter, aren't born this way. We don't come out of
the womb and get a rise at that first smack on the
ass. But the proclivity does exist in every living
creature.

It's that fight or flight impulse that kicks on when
the prey senses danger. That rush of adrenaline that
floods our system. For some, it's the rush and not the
danger or the pain that they seek. Still, they have to
go through the danger and the pain to get to that hit.

Domitia was a master at turning on that switch.

For decades, I watched her break down brutes and build up weaklings. When she was done with them, they all craved her nails at their throats, her heel in their back, her fangs in their hearts.

Carignan, the little gazelle in my snare isn't exactly weak. There is a strength to her, but it's buried deep. I can see it, right there behind the sadness in her eyes. Within her lies steel, a formidable spirit that would shine bright if she let it out.

I want to break her. I want to watch her face contort from the precipice of pain, only to dive into the abyss of ecstasy. I want to hear her scream from a high pitch that then reaches a low register of pleasure. I want to make her body twitch away from a cane or blade--no, a strap--only to inch closer when my tight knots loosen.

I want... her.

I back away from Carignan, breaking the trance I put her in. She blinks rapidly, trying to find her bearings. I do the same.

I have never wanted any woman but Domitia. Not even when I was a pubescent young man watching the grape pickers fornicate in my father's vineyard. I never lusted after one of the village girls. I always knew that something more awaited me.

That something, that someone, is not this daredevil damsel. Not a human with a death wish, because that's certainly what Carignan Durand's adventures will get her. Especially this latest venture of sitting before a starved vampire while the sweet scent of arousal wafts from between her thighs.

I could have her pussy stripped and bared in under a second. I doubt I'd need to compel her to do it. She wants it. Just as she wanted to tell me all her dark secrets.

Yes, she'd spill that honey right onto my fangs if I asked.

I wouldn't. I won't. I am just... amused that I can still get it up. Decades of nothing and now her.

The blood on her lip has dried. It's still warmer and fresher than what I drank from the bag earlier. I should clean that wound for her. She hasn't seemed to notice that she has split her lip. It's the least I can do.

I brush my thumb across her lip, gathering the small amount of fluid that breached her full bottom lip. Her pink tongue darts out and strikes my thumb.

Now it's my turn to blink rapidly. Now it's my turn to struggle to find my bearings. Now it's her spell that I am under.

My brain tells me to wipe the blood on my

trousers and not on my tongue. She is not for me. My victims are always faceless, their bodies just blood in a bag.

The monster in me wins out. Animal instincts bring my thumb to my mouth. My tongue latches on and takes every molecule of her blood. I swallow it down and my fangs sharpen.

I remember the first time I saw fireworks. The explosions had startled and then thrilled me. Carignan Durand's taste explodes in my mouth setting off tiny bombs of sense and sensation.

Her blood is tepid. If it was warm it would taste like ambrosia.

"I can't believe I just told you all that," she says.

I put my thumb behind my back like I'm a naughty little boy hiding the cookie he's just stolen from the cookie jar. "People say I have a trusting face."

Carignan narrows those honey-wine eyes at me. "No, they don't."

I can't help but like her. A little. "It'll be dawn soon. I need to get you home.

"You're sending me away?"

The pout on her face sparks something in my chest. "Do you want to stay?"

She scoots back on my bed, shifting the sheets

with the movement of her ass. Later, when she is gone, I will rest my face right in that spot. If I'm lucky, I'll dream of the sweet vineyard I could've run through between her thighs. Right now, it's as though she finally realizes she is prey.

"No," she says. "I just..." She hugs herself, rubbing at her forearms as though cold is settling in. "I don't want this feeling to go away."

Right. The sensations. The warmth of skydiving. The adrenaline that is still coursing through her veins because, unbeknownst to her, there is a monster that wants to devour her flesh.

"Maybe next time you'll do something safer," I say. "Like a plank walk."

"Plank walk? Like a pirate?"

"No," I grin. "Pirates are dangerous. There was a man who walked between two buildings some time ago. He was a Frenchman, so it can't be too dangerous."

I am joking. I haven't joked in centuries. The way she looks at me I can see that she is considering it.

"Don't." I put the command in my voice, but I sense her resistance.

I was right. Carignan is strong-willed. I enjoy her pushback for a second. I want to take a bite out of that supple ass of hers. I could string her up on my four-poster bed with the ropes she was wrapped in when she fell into my arms. I could suspend her wet pussy over my mouth and--

"You sound like my brother," she says.

"I am definitely not your brother." Not with the things I want to do to her. Things I hadn't even thought of for centuries.

Carignan wanted to be bound in a harness? She liked heights? She wanted to be pushed to the edge? Oh, the things I could do with her with the rope left from her failed parachute.

My dick is definitely hard now. Instead of tapping into that desire, shame washes over me. What am I doing desiring another woman when I failed to save the love of my life?

The possibility of death makes Carignan feel alive. But the thought of living another day makes me feel shame. The little daredevil and I are on different paths. Best I set her on her way.

I latch onto her eyes. She gazes back at me, not hiding what she's thinking, what she wants. She doesn't fight my suggestion this time. No, I fight my own resolution.

Still, I push the thought into her head. She is out in an instant. I catch her body before she hits the mattress. But have I made a new mistake?

Carignan is now helpless in my arms. I could do to her whatever I want. No one would know.

I rise with her in my arms as I walk to the head of the bed. Taking a seat, I settle down onto the mattress, cradling her in my lap, making sure to sit her away from my erection.

The crack in her lip offers no more sacrament. Her head rests against my chest. Her nose presses against the place my heart would be if I still had one. I don't know how long I sit there watching her breathe. The first rays of sunlight creep along the horizon when I reach for the phone and dial.

"I thought it would take you much longer to call."

There is delight in the voice on the other end. It makes my skin crawl. The creature on the receiving end of my call is the biggest predator in hundreds of miles.

"I need a favor," I say.

There is a soft chuckle. Likely the sound the lion makes before it takes down a buffalo. "I'll need something in return."

I hang up the phone. I should prepare her, but I am not yet ready to let her go. It would just be the one time I tell myself. I am a beast, after all. This is my nature.

I am a bastard for doing it. But I can't help

myself. I dip my head to hers. Gently, as tenderly as I know how, I take hold of her bottom lip with mine.

I do not bite. I do not suck. I simply press my lip to hers.

Carignan does not stir. This is no fairytale. She is Sleeping Beauty, but despite my moniker, I am no Prince. All I bring anyone is pain.

8

———

Cari

"The person who rides in the back seat does not have to be strapped in."

"Y-y-yes, they d-d-do."

My right eye twitches but doesn't open. I shift against my pillow but can't seem to get comfortable. The pillow is firm. And covered in leather and not the cotton liner I'd bought for it the other week. The television is too loud. Which is weird because I never sleep with it on.

"No, they doin't. Only them in the front."

What had I been watching before I'd fallen asleep? The BBC? Was Masterpiece Theater showing some period drama? It appeared to be something set in Scotland. Or maybe it was an Irish comedy? I'd never been any good with accents.

"I'm g-g-googling it."

Googling? There was no Google in the Victorian time period. Definitely not during the time of the highlanders.

Am I actually dreaming? Or is the television on AMC Classics? Yes, that has to be it. Because these men definitely don't sound like any rugged highlanders. They sound more like the Three Stooges or maybe the Three Leprechauns.

I hear the slaps and grunts of physical comedy as I struggle to come awake. When I open my eyes I don't see Larry, Curly, and Mo. What I'm seeing is just too weird to describe. And it's not on TV.

The sun is rising in the sky out the window. I'm in a car. A moving car.

In the front seat, the guy with the accent is in the driver's seat. Beside him, sits a tall, thin man. The thin man has his phone out, his slender fingers are tapping furiously over the face of the phone.

A man with gray hair, but a young face sits beside me in the backseat. He has his seat belt on. I look down to see that my belt is fastened securely across my chest. The gray-haired man gives me a weary smile.

"Th-th-there," says passenger seat guy. "It says it right here in G-g-google. Children up to s-s-sixteen must wear their b-b-belts."

"Is the lass over sixteen?" asks the driver.

The driver's gaze lifts and regards me in the rearview mirror. The man beside him turns his head, nearly all the way around without moving his shoulders, like a human owl.

"Well, are you, lass?" asks the driver.

"Of course she is," says the man beside me. "Do you think the Prince of Pain would tussle with a child?"

The two men in the front seat look dubious. I am utterly confused. Who is the Prince of Pain? Who are these three? How did I get here? Where are they taking me?

"I doin't know," says the driver. "Were those Hadrian's proclivities in the past?"

Hadrian.

The image of him rushes back to the front of my mind. His dark hair. His crystal clear green eyes. His sultry smile.

The memories flood back all at once. I bolt up, wide awake. The seat belt doesn't allow me to get too far. My body is alert and warm from just the mention of his name.

I fell from the sky. He caught me. He stared at my lips. And then... nothing.

The memories are jerky and jumbled from there. Did I tell him he made me feel warm? Did I lick his thumb? Oh god, what else did I do?

The last thing I remember is being with him, inside his arms. Feeling safe, secure, warm. So how did I wind up here kidnapped by these three stooges?

"Let me out," I demand.

"Don't worry, lass," says the driver. "We will."

Was this blackmail? Did they expect a ransom? My family is wealthy, but we've never been on the radar for kidnappers. Maybe this has something to do with my brother's political career? My sister has been in the papers with her scientific breakthroughs in grape hybrids.

"We're just a few miles away," says the man beside me.

"Where are you taking me?" I demand.

"To your apartment."

Wait? What? "You're kidnapping me to my own home?"

"No. No. We're driving you home from Hadrian's," says the man beside me. "He... well, he couldn't take you himself. So he asked us to do it."

"You're friends of Hadrian's?"

"No, not friends exactly. More like business associates...of his business associate."

That was a head-scratcher. But still, "Why would Hadrian send three men to take me home instead of calling an Uber?"

"You shouldna ever get into the car with strangers," says the driver, whose name I do not know and whose face I've never seen before.

I give him a telling look.

"We're entirely safe," the driver assures me.

They all nod earnestly. And I *am* wearing my seatbelt.

Did I fall asleep back at Hadrian's? It must have been the adrenaline from nearly dying, for real this time. I usually napped after any adventure sport.

I don't feel tired now. I'm still full of energy. I can't believe I fell asleep in front of Hadrian. No wonder he sent me away and asked his friends of friends to do it for him.

Man, I have no game when it comes to men. Never had. Maybe because I've never actually been interested in one before. Not any of the adrenaline junkies I hang with. Not the responsible instructors or guides. Not the safe boys in my prep school or the frat boys in college.

But after just a few moments with Hadrian and I had tingles all up and down my spine. Yes, it might have something to do with the fact that I fell into his arms after nearly dying. But the way he looked at me, like he saw straight into the heart of me. I've never experienced anything like that before.

There's still a tingle in my fingertips and on my bottom lip where he brushed his fingers. But the sensations are all fading away under the dawn's new light, like the sun's rays are burning them away.

"Tell me about him?" I ask no one in particular.

"Who? Hadrian? Trust us, lass. He's not exactly the kind of creature you want to get involved with."

"Creature?" I ask.

The backseat guy smacks the front seat guy in the back of the head. The driver takes his hand off the wheel to reach back and sock the gray-haired young man. The thin passenger seat man tries to break it up. Somehow we don't swerve into oncoming traffic.

"It's a figure of speech," says the driver once all things are settled down. "I'm Irish. Name's Declan, by the way."

"I'm Parker," says the guy beside me. "And that's

Laurie." He points to the passenger seat guy. "What Declan means is that Hadrian has certain... tastes that aren't for a girl like you."

"A girl like me?"

Laurie clears his throat and takes over the conversation. "I've heard of your f-f-family. Love Durand wine."

I have no interest in talking about wines. "I couldn't place Hadrian's accent. Was it Irish?"

"No." Declan scowls as though I've offended his entire country.

"My bad," I say, as innocently as I can muster. "You guys sound alike."

"Impossible. He's a Spaniard."

"No," says Parker. "He was born in Italy. Then he moved to Spain for... well, you know what."

Before I can ask what what, there is another round of smacking upside the head and over armrests. I try another tactic.

"So, he owned vineyards in Italy and Spain?" I ask.

"I believe his family was in the winemaking business," says Declan. "But he left the family business for many years. He's had other less savory jobs."

"Like what?" I prod. "Like the mafia?"

I am only half-joking. The silence is a definitive punch line. So that's what was up.

"Something like that," says Parker. "You'd best to keep your distance from the likes of him."

I bite my lip. There's the metallic taste of blood at the center of my bottom lip. But beneath the leaden taste is something sweet. "Well, we live in the same city. And his property is near my family's vineyard."

The three men look at one another again, sharing more silent communication. I can't get anything else out of them for the rest of the drive. We turn a corner and pull up to my brownstone.

"Here you are," says Parker. "All safe and sound."

"You're a good girl, lass," says Declan. "If Hadrian comes to your door, don't invite him in."

"If there's ever anything you n-n-need," says Laurie, "just give us a call."

I look up at the sky. A plane soars overhead. Before last night it would've called to me. In the light of the new day, I don't focus on the airplane. I focus on the buildings it flies above.

"Well," I say, "there is something. Have you ever heard of plank walking?"

9

_____

Hadrian

"Evening, Hadrian. Were you making Rocky Mountain Oysters for dinner again?"

I come into the kitchen to see my brothers already up and eating their evening meal. I don't answer Gaius, as my balls were spared from the sun's rays today. But my big toe did get burned.

"As a true connoisseur of *animelles*, you know I prefer bull testicles to four-hundred-year-old Italian meatballs," Gaius continues. "The organ is best when skinned, floured, with just a bit of salt and pepper. Then deep-fried to a golden crisp and pounded flat."

Gaius smacks his lips as he waxes poetic over the appetizer. He's dressed in a silk robe that likely cost more than a country village in France. His aristocratic nose is high in the air, even as it belies his low birth. His long lashes and dark eyes are perpetually narrowed so no one can ever tell if he's looking at them. Having known the man for half a millennium, I know he sees everything.

"We're out of B-Negative again," calls a voice from the kitchen.

Virius stands before the open, stainless steel refrigeration unit. The blond male who is built like his gladiator forefathers is dressed in a white toga around his hips, brown cowboy boots on his feet, and a motorcycle helmet with the visor up.

"Just drink the A-Negative," says Gaius.

"They taste nothing alike," Viri shouts through the open visor as he holds up the offensive A-Negative blood bag. "The B is bright and complex, with an earthy aftertaste. The A is sweet and creamy like sugar. You know I don't have a sweet tooth."

"Mix in some peppermint leaves. It contains iron and will give it an herby taste."

"Peppermint leaves?" Viri gags and tosses the bag back in the refrigerator. "That's like me telling you to toss back a glass of California Zinfandel."

Gaius presses his hand to his chest as though he were trying to keep the bile down. "No need to be crass. Just drink it. You both need to eat something before we go into polite society."

"Polite?" I ask. "Are you sure we're not walking into a firing squad?"

Gaius waves my comment away as though it is a gnat buzzing around his head. "What happened between Frangelico and Domitia was before our time."

I tense at the mention of her name. I know Gaius' hooded gaze catches my reaction. As always, he doesn't mention it.

"You should eat something, too," he says.

"I'm not hungry." I turn and head out of the kitchen.

"If you don't eat, you'll complain all the way there," Gaius calls after me. "I doubt Frangelico will have any bags on hand. Only live veins."

"I'll eat when we get there," says Viri.

"Are you gonna get dressed, buddy?" says Gaius.

I don't hear the rest of their conversation. However, the outcome is clear when we all exit the front door twenty minutes later. I'm in my typical wardrobe of black slacks and a black cotton shirt. Gaius is tailored to perfection in a dark blue business suit. Viri has lost the helmet and put on a colorful Hawaiian shirt. The boots and toga remain.

I take in the scenery as we drive the long, winding road that encompasses our new enterprise, the Serrano Vineyard in Patagonia. Our flagship vineyard back in Italy is two hundred years old and has earned us what amounts today to over a billion dollars. We need half that just to keep Gaius clothed and fed with his expensive tastes.

We've planted our signature Serrano grape in Spain, France, Switzerland, and even Australia. Arizona is the closest Gaius will come to the questionable soil of California. Gaius was loathe to mix our berries with the new technologies vintners on the west coast were toying with.

I didn't care. I needed a change of scenery. Too many ghosts back in the old country.

When we walk into our destination and take the private staircase down, I see a familiar scene. A woman spread eagle on the inverted cross of Saint Andrew. Her dark nipples are tight peaks that point to the ceiling. Her head lolls back in ecstasy as her master flails her naked skin.

Unbidden, the memory of my little skydiver rises in my mind. What would she look like stretched out on that cross? Or better yet, suspended in the air on ropes. Her body bound and completely at my mercy.

I shake my head to lose the thought. I'm not certain where the idea even came from. It isn't as though I'll ever see her again.

A row of bare asses salute us. Between the splayed legs are weeping pink cunts and leaking, erect dicks. Each cheek is stained pink as a leathered up Domme walks up and down the line taking a red-striped cane to the round flesh.

I am familiar with torture. I excel at it. Only, when I did it as an art form, it was not appreciated by the victims held in the Spanish dungeons awaiting judgment.

Beside me, Viri's stomach grumbles. I doubt he's remembering our time as henchmen in the Inquisition. No, his body's needs are of the present.

"I told you to eat before we came," hisses Gaius.

"I'm hungry now," Viri says. But his gaze isn't on the open play area. It's on the bar where I can smell that fresh B-Negative is on tap.

"You'll have to wait until the meeting is over," says Gaius.

Viri sucks his teeth, but he falls in line. We make our way through the moaning humans on the floor, those screaming upon vibrating furniture, and a few panting while suspended from ropes. At the end of the room are a dais and throne. Upon the throne sits the man we are here to see.

"*Salve*," calls Lucius Frangelico from his seat on the throne.

He doesn't stand. He is king here. He holds out his arm, palm down, fingers touching. The salute was a sign of respect in ancient times. The vampire king is offering an olive branch to us today.

He turns his palm over, and I see that I am mistaken. He curls his slender fingers in a come hither motion. In my hand I hold the favor he asked for; a bottle of wine from the old country, from a time when we were all centuries younger.

Frangelico's fingers curl around the bottle and his mouth splits into a true grin. The male has always made my skin crawl. Hopefully, this vintage bottle gets me out of his debt for the favor I asked of him last night.

"Nice touch," says Gaius when I step back.

He doesn't know that I had any recent contact with the Vampire King. I'd rather keep it that way. I don't need any questions about the little human I sent away the other night. I have no plans to ever see her again.

"As I'm sure you know, we purchased a vineyard on the outskirts of town," says Gaius. "It's beyond the boundary of your nest. But we still wanted to make sure we pay our respects."

Frangelico rubs his fingers over the ancient label. The wine is not only priceless, but it's also old. It was from my parents' vineyard, making it nearly four hundred years old. His shrewd eyes get a faraway look. For someone his age, I wouldn't be surprised if his eyes rolled back in his head. When he focuses back on us, his gaze is clear.

"My friends." Frangelico stands now and addresses the crowd. "We have royalty in our midst tonight. May I present the Prince of Pain, the Lord of the Lash, and the Knight of Knives."

Viri and I bristle at those monikers from our past. Gaius, on the other hand, does a turn so that his admiring audience gets a good look at him. In turn, I see Gaius' hooded gaze take in the interested.

Most of the humans in the room are too blissed out to know what is happening. It's only the vampires and few shifters that take note. They are the only beings old enough to know what those names mean; names whispered in dark alleys, names groaned in rank dungeons, names screamed for mercy during the Spanish Inquisition.

"As you can see," says Frangelico, "your reputation precedes you."

"It's our shared past that concerns us," I say.

I'm usually the quiet one. I have no head or patience for diplomacy. That's why Gaius does all the talking for our business.

Frangelico's gaze lands on me. Like Gaius, his scrutiny is laser-sharp. Unlike Gaius, Frangelico's unblinking eyes do not squint. I have his full, wide attention.

He knows who I am. More importantly, he knows who I loved.

"The past is dead," says Frangelico.

The hairs at the back of my neck bristle. My fingers itch to clench into fists. My fangs ache to pierce through my gums.

Gaius steps in front of me with a congenial grin. "Let not the sins of our sire be laid upon her sired. If that were the lay of the land, you'd be a dead man."

Frangelico's icy glare switches from me to Gaius. His predatory smile turns into something approaching friendly, as friendly as the smile of the scorpion who climbed upon the turtle's back to cross the river. That story ends in a murder-suicide.

"Well said, my lord," says Frangelico. "If I were

held responsible for every dirty deed of my sireds, I'd have been roasting in the sun for a year."

My fingers do ball into a fist now. But thoughts of hurting Frangelico leave my mind. What fills my vision is my last sight of Domitia. Her beautiful face in tears. Her hands reaching for me, begging me to come with her.

But I don't. I didn't, and she slipped through my fingers as the sun's rays consumed her body.

"We'd love to see your handiwork for ourselves," Frangelico is saying as I come back to the present.

I blink, adjusting to the lighting in the dungeon. Looking around the large open space, I see many eager women and a few males. But I no longer deal in pain. Not since the woman I loved died.

"My friends will join you," I say. "I'll be out of your way."

I have no interest or desire to socialize or be a part of paranormal politics. I just want to be left alone with my grapes at night and wake early at dusk to give a middle finger to the setting sun.

Gaius has already picked up a flogger. Viri is at the bar placing his order. I head for the door, but a hand stops me.

I turn to see Frangelico. "I can't say that I am

sorry for your loss, being that Domitia tried to turn my sireds against me, steal all my wealth, and stake me. But I truly harbor no ill will to you."

"Thank you for the loan of your shifters," I say. "I consider any debt between us paid and I'll trouble you no longer."

"You know," Frangelico continued as though I had not spoken, "I have everything in the world. But the one thing I lack is a true brotherhood like the three of you have."

I look back at my brothers. We were born of different mothers in our human lives. But Domitia's blood runs through each of our veins as the woman who gave us new life. Gaius, Virius, and I stuck by each other through the dark ages instead of killing each other off like many of Frangelico and his contemporaries. But I don't bother mentioning that.

"Maybe one day we could even be friends. Fates know I could use a few after dealing with that Aleron problem."

I can only stare. Frangelico's fingers on my shoulder feel like a scorpion's bite. I shake off his touch.

Frangelico shrugs, undaunted and unconcerned. One on one he would best me. He has over a millennium on me.

"If you ever have need again, don't hesitate to reach out."

Frangelico hands me a card with his name, a phone number, and an email address on it. For a man who guards his safety, he sure has a lot of ways to get in touch. I don't want to be in touch. I just want to be left alone.

I am not the only one who desires to leave this place in a hurry and untouched. A tall man bumps into me on his way to the door. The human male turns to glare at Frangelico. I note that his eyes are the color of Chianti and I'm suddenly thirsty.

Not for him. When I did drink from veins I preferred my victims cowering in fear or screaming in pain. This man's back is so rigid, his walks so stiff, I'm certain a stick is shoved way up his ass. He'd certainly taste like cold, unsweet, black coffee from a convenience store at best.

Not like the little human who I let escape my grasp the other night.

"Leaving so soon, Durand?" Frangelico calls after the man. "Was it something I said?"

Durand? Chianti colored eyes? I turn to ask Frangelico about the man, but his shrewd gaze has left the man and taken up interest in me.

I clamp my mouth shut and school my features.

Whatever is happening here is none of my concern. Frangelico smirks at me, but he says nothing as I head out into the oblivion of night. I am determined never to ask the man for so much as the time of day ever again.

10

Cari

The first ray of sunlight hits my cheek. The morning is cold. The star isn't up high enough to warm me through.

Not that I could feel it in any case.

I open my eyes to see a beautiful day dawning. At 18,000 feet in the air, the view is spectacular. The sky is full of pinks and purples and oranges, like an artist dropped their paintbrushes on the floor.

Huh? That's good to know. Though I'm an unfeeling thing, I can still paint a pretty picture with my words.

I look down and my breath catches. Finally, a

spark of something in me. A slight jostle in this walking corpse that is my body. The shaky breath tells me I'm still alive.

Height: it's the only thing that wakes up my senses. That and speed. Hence, being over three miles up in the air preparing to step out and take a walk on this glorious, sunny morning. Although, I would rather be in the arms of a certain tall, dark glass of wine with a proclivity to catch things that fall from the sky.

"OMG, what am I doing?" The girl next to me squeals. She's a talking texter, so I only understand about half of what she says.

"WTF though. Sometimes you just gotta YOLO."

I nod at her nonsensical abbreviations. I feel as though I'm being treated as a child by an adult who spells out the bad words. I'm pretty sure she's older than me. Her hair is a riot of neon rainbow coloring, so bright it actually hurts to look at.

"We'll be LMFAOing after this, right, Cari?" she says as she grips her pack.

Instead of talking, I raise both my thumbs. I've learned silence doesn't shut her up. I'm sure she's one of those chronic texters that will keep bubbles popping up until the other person responds. The only thing that works with a chronic texter is an emoji. Hence the head nod and thumbs up.

I step away from her wishing there was more space. My fingers are numb as I pull at my restraints. I am strapped down tight. I won't be escaping anytime soon. All the sensation I felt yesterday after waking from my time with Hadrian has gone. I've come up into the sky because I need a fix and I need it bad.

The binds cross my spine, pulling my back straight. They crisscross over my breasts. The straps reach around my thighs, riding up to my crotch like a lover's caress. Or, perhaps, a possessive grip. Much like it had felt when Hadrian had carried me through his vineyard and into his bedroom. My nipples had strained for his touch.

I am not flat-chested, though the straps do their best to flatten my girls. My nipples press into my mounds. It's not erotic. But I do feel high. I am high.

Beside me, I hear a snort.

"Sup, Cari."

Tate wipes a speck of powder off his nose and gives me a cheeky grin. He is my age, but he looks much older. There is a strain to the light in his eyes. A permanent wrinkle mars his brow.

Tate has been on most of these adrenaline

adventures with me. From bungee jumping to base jumping, from zip-lining to diving with sharks. We've done just about all of it. But for different reasons.

Tate is trying to forget his past. I'm trying to remember mine.

"You ready for this?" he asks.

I nod. Then remember I'm not speaking to Chronic Texter. "Yeah. You?"

"Always," he says, giving me a wink.

I know he's interested in me. But sleeping around isn't a risk I'm willing to take. Well, maybe with Hadrian. But definitely not with Tate the Druggie Daredevil. Condoms are probably an afterthought for a guy who engages in behaviors that could end his life.

"You look nervous," he says.

I'm not. I'm eager. Eager to get started. Eager to feel the wind on my face. To feel the air slip through my fingers. To feel the pressure drop and my heart rate increase. I am just eager to *feel*.

The two others who are with us, Chronic Texter and her porcelain skinned, kohl-eyed, black nail polish boyfriend, are both attached to tandem divers. Tate and I aren't. Like I said, it isn't our first rodeo. This is a weekly occurrence for us. While Tate was snorting up his feelings, sometimes I came twice a week. This is my drug of choice.

Not that I do any drugs. My therapist tried putting me on meds after our third session when I told her about my latest hobby of drag racing. I thought that was pretty ludicrous since she'd been the one to suggest exposure therapy in the first place.

True, she only prescribed getting in the car with a driver. Her thought was to get me back behind the wheel after the accident. What I noticed was that it wasn't driving that scared me. Nothing scares me. That is the problem.

I wait now for the others to jump, wanting a bit of the sky to myself. The Chronic Texter's and Goth Guy's panicked screams have died away. Tate's war cry echoes in my ears. And then there is silence. Just me in the clouds.

After my mom died, my dad told me she was in heaven. When I asked where that was he pointed up. I've looked up into the sky since I was a little girl and I've never seen her. But she died when I was five, so I barely remember what she looked like.

I've been coming up here for the last six months. Flying through the clouds where he told me Heaven was. But I haven't seen him either.

I step to the edge of the open doorway. I know this is crazy after what happened last night. There is a tinge of fear, but it's the anticipation that pushes me forward. Usually, I hope to hear my dad's voice in my head. To feel his arms around me as the air pushes back at my falling body. I take a deep breath and close my eyes. When I do, that's when I see Hadrian's face.

The wind hits me in the chest as I tumble through the sky. I don't fight gravity. I learned that being tense only brings pain whether you're slamming into another vehicle at sixty miles per hour, or falling through the sky at one hundred and twenty miles per hour.

And so I let go. I let go of it all. All the responsibilities I want no part of. All the cares I no longer have. All the fucks I no longer give.

The free fall continues. I know the clock is ticking. I have less than a minute before I need to deploy the chute.

Thirty seconds pass as I tumble through the sky. A bright light flashes in my eyes. It's not Hadrian's Italian tenor in my ear. I hear my dad's voice.

Forty seconds pass and I continue to accelerate. In my mind's eye, I see my dad pump the brakes of the car. But it doesn't matter.

Fifty seconds have passed as I free-fall down to the ground. The crash sounds in my ears. My father moans a sigh and then his final words.

Get free, Carignan. Live.

The wind whips about me, trying to knock some sense into my thick skull. I'm a good girl. A daddy's girl. I do what I'm told.

Finally, my fight or flight responses engage. My heart rate increases. Blood pumps through my sluggish veins.

Conscious thought turns off. My reflexes click in. My adrenaline spikes. I imagine it's like a shot of pure, undiluted heroine. I should ask Tate. He would know.

My eyes slam open. I grip my harness. My fingers search for the pull and I give it a yank.

My breath catches, wondering if it will open this time. Wondering if I want another accident. Wondering if I want to hit the ground or fall back into strong arms.

There is a jerk as the chute deploys. My harness tightens around me. It tugs at the V of my thighs, the straps giving my ass a swat. It heaves over the flesh of my breasts, giving my nipples a firm pinch.

I sail through the air in this tight cocoon of sensation. Sensations that zing up and down my legs. My breath comes in short, needy pants. I feel alive.

But the ground is fast approaching. It never lasts long enough. Already, my senses are going dull. My fingertips are numbing. My toes feel detached. Paralysis spreads down my spine. And my mind, my heart, they're becoming indifferent once more.

I kick my feet out, coming to a running stop. The fabric of the parachute falls around me, like a funeral shroud. It's over.

I am the walking dead again. I am a senseless woman. I am a lifeless corpse that survived a crash without a scratch while her father's spine was broken in three places along with massive internal damage.

In the distance, I can see Chronic Texter is tangled with her tandem diver. There are scrapes on her cheek and forehead. Her goth boyfriend moans as he holds his foot. It's likely broken. Tate takes a tumble, adding to his collection of bruises.

Once again, I walk away unscathed.

11

———

Hadrian

I pull open the stainless steel refrigerator. The day workers we hired have restocked the shelves. The top shelf is filled with O-positive; the most common blood type of humanity. On the second shelf, there's a large stash of A-negative bags; the second most common of blood donors. In the pull out shelves which are reserved to keep fruits and vegetables crisp is a small supply of B-negative, one of the rarer blood types.

Taking a bag from the crisper, I marvel at this modern convenience of humanity. Refrigeration units are one of the few human technologies I actually enjoy. In ancient times we could never store blood outside of a live body. At least not for long. Especially not without keeping said body incapacitated.

Vampires prefer to drink from the living. When the heart stops, the blood coagulates and the consistency of the fluid becomes curdled. Much like cheese. But trust me, topping fresh fruit with clotted blood like humans do cottage cheese is not a thing for vampires.

I pour the blood bag into a coffee mug and toss it into the microwave. As I detest the taste of cold blood, the little electric oven is another favorite technological advance. Even though the radiation does make the blood taste a little funny. But it's my only option. It's too easy to scorch blood on the stovetop. Plus I hate what blood does to the pots and pans and the dishwasher.

After the beep, I remove my warmed mug. It's a bit too hot. Burning the tip of my tongue would be an annoyance that would heal in a matter of seconds, but I am thirsty. So, I blow off the steam for a few seconds before it's safe to take my first sip.

Before putting the cup to my lip, I bless the blood. Old habits die hard. I was ordained when I became an inquisitor. First by Pope Sixtus and again by Pope Paul IV.

In the old days, I feasted on heretics as I tore their flesh with whips, canes, and flails. Fear and desperation gave the blood a sweet taste, like honey wine. When a victim screamed, the blood became savory. When they wept, there was a tartness to it. But fear, fear was my favorite dish.

Humans have tortured each other since the beginning of time, all the way back to Cain. Life as a vampire wasn't hard in the middle ages with persecutions aplenty. During the Spanish Inquisition, the blood flowed in the dungeons.

I cared not for confessions, as was my charge. I went to work solely for my sustenance. If I didn't like the way someone tasted, they were guilty. If I wanted seconds at their veins, I told my superiors the accused was being stubborn and needed more time in the dungeons until I drained them dry. Only then did I turn them over for final punishment.

Burning at the stake was a mercy by the time I was done with them. Vampires didn't cry over spilled milk. But we would get put out over burned blood.

Unfortunately, the blood from the microwave is tangy, like champagne. I cringe at the thought of the bubbly monstrosity. Packaged blood is still better than that excuse of liquid. This donor was probably some sorority girl or junior executive who drank Cosmos every happy hour.

"Good evening, Hadrian."

Gaius comes into the room dressed in the same slacks he wore last night and a few buttons missing on his designer shirt. There's a fading scratch on his chest which could've only come from a shifter. Somehow I doubt he got into a fistfight last night.

"You're up late today."

Gaius' meaning is clear. He hopes I missed my morning bout with the sun. If he looked down and saw the singe on my pinkie toe he'd know he was wrong. "You were out late. I'm surprised you trusted Frangelico to not turn you out at high noon."

"Lucius never had any quarrel with us."

"Oh, it's Lucius now? What else? Did you two braid each other's hair at your sleepover?"

Gaius pops the cork of our signature wine and pours himself a glass. "Domitia made a lot of enemies when she was alive. Many of them were before our time. You don't need to hold her grudges."

"You want me to break bread with a man who tried to kill her."

"She did start it."

I grit my teeth. It is always how these arguments go. Domitia did steal the queen's jewels, so no wonder the guards came after her. Domitia did double-cross the pirate, so no wonder the fleet came after her. Domitia did try to assassinate the Pope, so no wonder we had to give up being Inquisitors.

"It's been over two hundred years, brother. Perhaps it's time to move on."

This was always the next progression of the argument. "Death does not stop true love. It says so in that Dread Pirate Roberts movie."

"Domitia was no Buttercup," Gaius snorts. Then immediately winces. He holds up his hands in defense before I can get my hands around his neck. "I loved her, too."

"No, you didn't."

"No," he agrees, lowering his hands. "I didn't. I am grateful to her for the life she gave me. Including my new family. But she made her choice. She walked into the sun."

He was wrong again. It wasn't her choice. It was my fault. I was supposed to save her and I failed.

"You're still alive," Gaius continues. He stands and places a hand on my shoulder. His hand is a firm grip, as though he's determined to root me into this world. "One day you'll have to start living again."

I move to shrug him off. But my shoulders are too weary. My eyes feel heavy and I can't meet his gaze. He doesn't know what happened the day Domitia faced the sun. I never told anyone.

Viri lumbers into the kitchen. He glances at the two of us. His only acknowledgment is a slight head nod.

This morning he is dressed in Victorian pantaloons, an AC/DC t-shirt covering his chest, and a pair of Air Jordans on his feet. He pulls open the fridge and goes for the crisper. His hand pauses over the supply.

"Who's been in my stash?" says Viri.

"You know I don't drink from the tap." Gaius returns to his seat and his wine glass.

Viri turns to me. I can't deny it. Not when the evidence is still in my hand.

"You know that's my favorite," he says.

"I'll replace it," I say, downing the last tart droplet.

"That's not the point," says Viri. "I put my initials on it."

"Oh?" I frown. "I thought that was the donor."

"I need to move out and get my own place." Viri slams the door of the fridge shut, cradling the lot of B-negative bags in his arms.

Fat chance he'll move out. Viri is barely a functioning member of the paranormal world. He would never pass for anything close to human. Not when he couldn't even get the fashions of the century correct.

"Children," says Gaius. "Can we talk shop for a minute?"

I take a seat beside Gaius. Viri begins opening blood bags and dumping the contents into a thermos.

"I'm growing concerned about the soil content here," says Gaius. "Our grapes aren't progressing as they should."

What has kept Serrano grapes a top wine for centuries is the consistency of the taste. Our berries are the exact same from my parents' vineyard from four hundred years ago. The grapes were the only thing in my life, aside from my blooded brothers, that haven't changed.

"I'm worried the soil and the temperature are changing the taste," said Gaius.

I feel a discussion of soil pH, fertilization methods, and vine health coming on. Even though I grew up on a vineyard, handling the grapes was not my job. Nor my passion.

Gaius was born a slave. After Domitia turned us, Gaius took his newfound freedom and his knowledge of vinting to amass an empire. An empire he could wax quixotic upon for hours.

"That's not our department," I say, rising before he can get going. "You'll figure it out."

"Fine," says Gaius, glaring at my disinterest. "Just have the new barrels ready. And make sure the destemmers are clean for the harvesting."

"Since when do I not do my job?" says Viri around a mouthful of blood.

Gaius threw up his hands, clearly finished with the both of us. "My work here is done. I'm headed back to Club Toxic."

"You just got home," I say.

"Wasn't aware I had a curfew, Dad."

I give him a two-fingered salute, the Roman sign for fuck you.

Gaius rolls his eyes and straightens the cuffs of his crumpled shirt. "Fine. I'm off to the land of the living. You two can stay here stuck in the past."

Works for me. And, by the looks of Viri's Air Jordans kicked up on the table, it works for him, too.

12

———

Cari

Speed limits. They were just a suggestion. Right?

The sign mentioning fifty miles per hour whizzes past me as the needle of the speedometer crosses over eighty miles per hour.

I press the gas pedal of my car. The flip-flop I'm wearing dangles. It's being held between my big toe and the second one –what's that one called? The index toe? The pointer pinkie? It's not like it points to anything.

I know driving with open-toed and open-heeled shoes can be dangerous. There's always the possibility of the sandal footgear slipping between the toe thumb and the index toe and getting wedged under the accelerator. Or the brake. Which would be dangerous. Especially at excessive speeds.

A yellow sign indicating a bend in the road barely comes into focus before it's miles behind me. A second sign, indicating lowered speed is hazy as well. I take the curve with one hand on the steering wheel. The other checks the text messages popping up on my phone.

Up ahead a semi enters the highway. The driver is minding the speed limit. I should call the number on the back of his truck and let his boss know that his driving is indeed good.

Instead, I take my time running my foot from the gas pedal to the brake of my Miata. The pavement between me and the sixteen wheeler is decreasing but not my speed. My flip flop dangles between my toes.

The sixteen wheeler is in front of me now. Close enough that its wheels kick dirt directly on my windshield. A few of the tiny rocks strike my cheek. A few specks get into my hair because the top of my convertible is down.

I can smell the exhaust of the diesel fuel. I can

hear the tinkling of tiny rocks rain down on the hood of the car. The paint job is probably scratched.

I jerk when the blow horn of the semi sounds into the night. It breaks me from my numbness and I brake, hard.

My chest jams into the steering wheel as the speedometer flatlines. Seatbelts are just a suggestion, too. Right?

My chest colliding with the steering wheel doesn't hurt, much. Not much can hurt me anymore. I am invincible.

I pull off my exit. As I slow the car, my heartbeat kicks up. It doesn't race. It's probably beating at a regular click, like a normal person's.

Looking out the windshield, something approaching warmth fills my chest. There are vines as far as the eye can see. They are arranged in neat rows. Equidistant apart. Equidistant in height.

My father would have it no other way. He was meticulous about this vineyard. When he wasn't at the breakfast table in the morning, he could be found out in the vineyard, picking grapes before the first worker showed up.

Gazing out at the fruit of his labors brings me joy. Though the feeling is only lukewarm. My emotions are a tea kettle left on a cool burner. I need a spark to heat them up.

But I'm on the ground, going at a normal speed. There's no match down on the ground. There's no fire sitting still.

Still, I hold onto the tiny ember of joy the memory brings me. My dad used to walk me through the rows on his shoulders. He was a tall man. So I got a bird's eye view of the red and purple of the berries set against the brown of the vines in the sea of green leaves.

"Good, you're here." My sister Marechal comes up to my parked car.

I can't remember parking. I barely remember the drive here. I get out and allow her to hug me, wishing I could feel her warmth.

Mare is always warm. When she let me sleep in her bed as a little girl, I would always kick off the covers and snuggle into her side. We haven't slept in the same bed for over ten years.

Mare is ten years older than me. I was one of those surprise babies, had later in life when my mother was in her forties. Another impossible feat I'd come through.

Mare looks me up and down. She wears a tailored business skirt showcasing her curves, a buttoned-up blouse more than hinting at her D cups, and Louboutins at her feet lengthening her already long legs. She would look like a hot librarian, except for the lab coat over her ensemble. That white coat and the prescription glasses turn her into every nerd's fantasy of a sexy scientist.

After the hug, Mare doesn't let me go. She tilts my chin up and delivers a double-cheeked kiss. We are second-generation American, but you couldn't take the French out of our veins if you tried.

"Arneis and the lawyers are here," she says. "The sooner we get this done, the better. I've got a mountain of lab work. You ready?"

Mare takes my hand like we are a united front. Her expensive heels click on the floors as we head through the house into our dad's old study. My flip-flops clack the marbled floors of my childhood home.

"I don't see why you guys even need me," I say.

"Papa left us equal shares in the vineyard."

I didn't deserve the share of the empire my father had built. Not when I was the reason it's all come crumbling down.

"Just let them know you want to keep the vineyard running," Mare says. "You want to keep it in the family. You know what this place meant to Papa. We can get it back to its glory again. Wait until you taste my new wine mix."

I always let Mare boss me around. I idolized her when I was a little girl. I wanted to do everything she did. Be everything she was. But I am not.

I suck at science. I have no head for numbers. And I screw up everything I touch, yet always seem to come out unscathed. Case in point, I'm responsible for my father's death, but neither of my siblings seems to blame me.

My father's old study looks the same as the last time I was in here, for the reading of the will. It's even filled with the same people. They asked me questions then, questions I was too scarred to answer. Now my time is up.

"Hey, *ma petite fille*." My big brother Arneis pulls me in for a hug. He does not bother with the two kisses. He's fully assimilated into American life. So much so that he's taken office in the local government.

Arneis pulls me aside, away from Mare and the lawyers. "I know you've had a rough time this year. But it's almost over. Say the word and you don't have to deal with any of this anymore. We can sell the vineyard and make a nice profit to set you up so you don't have to do anything for the rest of your life."

Arneis wants to sell the vineyard. Marechal wants to keep it going. Me? I don't care one way or the other. But it all comes down to my vote.

No matter what I decide, someone I love will get hurt and I will walk away without a scratch. Again.

Arneis takes a seat on one side of me and pats my knee. Mare sits on the other side and rubs my arm. The suits begin talking technical legalese that goes over my head. Because I am in over my head.

I'm walking on a tight rope between the last two pillars of my foundation. My balance is precarious. At any moment I'll fall off. Would there be anyone there to catch me? Perhaps a green-eyed man who makes me want to spill all of my secrets?

"Carignan? What's your decision?"

13

___

Hadrian

I wrap my bare hands around a cherry tree. With a heave I uproot it. With my nails, I cut the tree's top above the last branch. My skin tears and chaffs. I don't ignore the pain. It's part of my process.

When the work of picking grapes became back-breaking for me as a young man, I moved on to become a cooper, the person who crafts the barrels that help give the wine its distinct flavor. It isn't just what grows on the vine that gives flavor. It's also how the wood is chosen, how it is fired, and molded into shape to hold the wine.

Oak was the tried and true wood for barrels. But

I wanted to try cherry bark here in Patagonia. I also experimented with hickory, maplewood, chestnut, and walnut. I heard of Japanese winemakers using cedar for a minty taste. That was a step too far.

I love pounding the wood, the smell of the bark toasting over the fire. It is a lost art. I have heard tell some winemakers put their wine into cardboard boxes to serve. Where is the Inquisition when you need it?

Using the edge of my hand like a blade, I split the wood into quarters that will become the staves that will create the shape of the barrel. I dig my fingers into the wood, shaping the staves into the curved dimensions I want. With that done, I put the pieces into the cellar to dry. There they'll stay for three years so that the wood is waterproof. Wine-making is a long game. The three of us have nothing but time.

The machines are all clean, meaning Viri is done for the night. He is a cellar rat. He does all the grunt work below the ground that transforms the grapes into liquid ambrosia. Like me, he prefers to work in solitude. Life has not been kind to either of us in the love department.

I walk past the ancient torture devices which have been shoved into the corner. But as I walk by I get a vision of a body being stretched over the rack. Dark nipples straining as her back bends. Honey-wine eyes wide as the pleasure wracks through her body.

I bring my thumb to my mouth for the tenth time tonight. Her taste is long gone, but the memory lingers. No, that's not true. My thoughts of her replace my first taste of honey or cherries. She becomes the new litmus test by which I will judge a dessert.

"You thinking of her?"

I look up to find Gaius. He's out of the denim work clothes he wears when he works with the grapes. He stands before me in slacks and an expensive shirt.

Am I that transparent? I wasn't aware he saw Carignan earlier the other evening. Perhaps those shifters Frangelico sent over woke him. Or perhaps Frangelico told Gaius about the favor I asked of him.

"It's been two hundred years, Hadrian."

Oh. He isn't talking about the human. He's talking about Domitia, my one true love.

"I've tried to hold my tongue for the last two centuries, but I think it's time you move on."

"Move on?" I turn the words over in my mouth. They don't taste as bitter as they should.

"I know you believe she was the love of your life…"

The way he rolls his eyes and sighs at the end of his sentence belies his assertion.

"But your relationship with Domitia was tumultuous on its best days. Turbulent on the normal days. Homicidal on the worst days."

I would be the first to admit Domitia and I had our ups and downs. But that is how passion works. Love is a raging storm, not a calm sea.

"I know we've never talked about this." Gaius comes up to me and puts his hand on my shoulder. "Men didn't talk about things like this in our time. Hell, they don't talk about these things today."

"What things?"

"You are an abuse survivor."

I knock his hand off my shoulder. That is just too far. "She and I both enjoyed it rough. You of all people should know that."

Despite what the religious books might say, monogamy wasn't as prized a relationship status in ancient times. Domitia certainly didn't believe in the practice. She had many lovers, including Gaius and Viri and an army of others. Literally. She once boarded a warship for the Spanish Armada and offered herself up to any sailor who was willing.

Me? I suppose I was ahead of my time. I was faithful from the beginning to the end.

"A good flogging," says Gaius, "sure. A bit of choking and breath play, fine. But staking you?"

"That was one time."

Gaius raises a brow.

"Fine," I admit. "Twice."

Domitia had partially staked me a couple of times during arguments. But she had never twisted the stake or sent it all the way through to actually kill me. She was a passionate woman given to fits of jealousy. Even though I'd never given her cause to doubt my devotion.

She could sleep with an army. She could bed my friends. But she did not take well to me looking at another woman. Not that I ever did. I am devoted to this day.

The image of Carignan comes into my mind. Her eyes that sparkle like a glass of fine wine. Her smile that has no bite. Her worry that she caused me pain.

"She was your first and only," Gaius is saying. "She shouldn't be your last. You should know what a normal relationship feels like."

"Says the man who's had a different woman in his bed every night for five centuries."

"Blasphemy," Gaius spits. "I don't sleep in a bed."

I try not to crack a smile. But he knows me too well. He chuckles first and I follow suit.

It is a miracle that we are friends, brothers. I tried to kill him a few times after Domitia took him to bed. We were equally matched and always came away bloody and bruised. A few times he had me at his mercy, but he never delivered the kill strike with a stake to my heart. When I finally got the better of him, I found I couldn't pierce his chest. The bastard grew on me, and I came to see that he didn't love Domitia.

The relationship between a sire and their sireds is a tricky beast. Most sires are murdered by their children. Perhaps that's why Domitia only ever turned young men. We were all putty in her hands.

But still, "Abusive?" I say. "I wasn't some simpering flower, Gaius. I loved her."

His hooded gaze quirks, missing nothing.

"Love her." I quickly correct my tense.

"You had it right the first time, brother. It's all in the past. She's gone. You should let her go."

That is exactly the problem. That's what I did. We had a fight, the worst we'd had in decades. I was prepared to walk away. But not forever.

I'd let her go that night. By daybreak, she was nothing but ash. All because of another jealous fit.

"She stepped out into the sun," says Gaius. "We'll never know why."

No, that wasn't true either. I did know why. I knew, but I didn't reach her in time.

"All I'm saying is she fucked you in the head," says Gaius. "You might as well actually get fucked. Come out with me tonight."

My dick stirs at the thought of fucking. But not some nameless sub at Club Toxic. I don't want to go out. I want to stay home and look at the sky. Maybe prowl around the vineyards within the vicinity waiting for something to fall from the sky.

"Not tonight," I say. "I have work to do, a phone call to make."

"I tried." Gaius throws up his hands. But he embraces me in a one-armed hug.

I return the gesture. He is the reason I made it out of the darkness of the Middle Ages.

I wait until I hear the engine of his car roar to life before I lift the phone. Only to put it back down a second later as Viri walks by.

The male is in faded jeans and ruffled tunic. There was a B-negative blood bag in one hand. A whiskey bottle in the other.

He nods at me. It is the only acknowledgment

he'll give me for the rest of the night. He is a true lost cause. Maybe I want to be found.

I dial. I don't waste time on pleasantries when the other end is picked up. "Was the package delivered safely the other day?"

"We took her home."

Well, that was that. I had no reason to check on her. There was always the awkwardness of having to be invited inside a human's home.

"But she did ask us for a favor."

"What favor?"

"She said she wanted to plank walk. So we helped her arrange something."

Fuck. So she wasn't done toying with her own life. Well, if Carignan was going to be careless with it he'd just have to take charge of it himself.

14

———

Cari

I learned there is an actual plank walk. Not the one Hadrian was talking about. That one happened in New York with a Frenchman known as Philippe Petit. I think Hollywood made a movie about it.

The actual plank walk is in China. It's known as the world's most dangerous hiking trail; Mount Huashan. The Road in the Sky.

I saw pictures of it during my Googling after my comedic escort home. I couldn't get to sleep after my skydiving adventure earlier in the day. I was far too keyed up. I'm not used to having that much energy and I had no idea what to do with all that vitality.

Well, that's not true. I knew what I wanted to do with it. But the man I wanted to do something with it about hadn't contacted me. His contact info wasn't listed in the phone book, or anywhere on the internet. And the three stooges wouldn't give it to me, no matter how much I offered them. But they did say they could do something about the plank walk.

So, while I waited, I fired up my laptop. Instead of searching out porn sites and looking for scenes containing dark-haired men with green eyes tying up girls, I searched for the term Hadrian had mentioned to me.

The Mount Huashan Road in the Sky is a series of ancient paths chiseled into the mountainside. The planks are suspended on cliffs with crisscrossing wooden planks only inches wide with narrow footholds and steep stairs made of stone. All that is there for security are rusty chains bolted into the mountainside as handholds.

Or at least that's how it used to be. From the pictures I saw from my search, there are cable cars and harnesses at the site now. It's been transformed for the safety of tourists who wanted life-altering excursions, but not a life-ending experience. I struck it from my bucket list.

Seat belts are a suggestion in my life.

"You sure about this?" Tate's fingers tap a nervous rhythm on the brick wall. Most of his nails are jagged lines, gnawed down to the nub. He chews at his cuticles now.

I look out before me and my heart kicks up a beat. It's not a mountain that I'm about to traverse. But the two structures below me are high in the sky.

There is construction underway at the old Patagonia Savings and Trust building and the Robles High Rise. These two towering structures are only 1300 feet in the air. Not exactly the Twin Towers that Philippe Petit walked between the roofs of. But those buildings aren't an option any longer.

There is a wide plank that is now stretched between the two roofs. The two buildings are also closer together than the New York towers were. The plank stretches less than a quarter-mile. Not impossible, but still dangerous enough to get the blood pumping in my veins.

The stooges worked fast to get the plank laid. I'd paid them a ransom's worth to do it. There is a harness there that they insisted on. I wear it. But only because I like the feel of the bindings criss-crossing my body.

"You can go back down if you want," I say to Tate.

"No, no," he says, spitting out the bit of flesh he's torn from his thumb's nail bed. "I told you, danger gives me a boner."

I turn to him, looking at him as though I'm seeing him for the first time. He looks like he's aged since this morning. He's just a few years older than me, twenty-five I think he told me. But he looks at least ten years older than that. His hair is thinning. There are wrinkles all around his eyes and mouth. He looks like he is in a mid-life crisis trying to recapture his youth.

He tugs a vial from his pocket. Inside is the white powder that is stealing his youth. "Want a hit?"

"Nah," I say, turning down the coke. "I'm good."

I never want anything interrupting the natural high. If I am impaired, I might miss the sensations. I want to wake up my feelings, not deaden them.

I tune out Tate's snort and focus on what I'm about to do. There is a hum of anticipation in my body. Probably what Tate feels every time he goes to his dealer to score.

I inhale and smell the fresh, clean scent of night air. The breeze kicks up and my stomach flutters, my gut knows it's about to get fed. The moon shines on my face, a spotlight as I take my place on the wooden stage that is a twelve-inch wide plank secured between two rooftops.

When I pull the straps of my harness tight, I get a tingle all over my skin. When I lock myself into the apparatus, my heart starts to pound. When I step onto the plank, I go breathless.

The wind lifts the tiny hairs on the nape of my neck. The air up here is thinner. Not as cold and thin as standing in the open door of a plane ready to jump. But similar enough. My nerves wake up.

It isn't as warm as my head against his chest. It isn't as sizzling as his fingertips on my lips. The hold of the harness isn't as tight as being in his arms. The light of the moon doesn't ignite me like his breath on my forehead did.

Why am I up here and not on Hadrian's doorstep?

Because he knows who I am. He knows where I live. He could've come to me anytime today. He could've called to check and see if I was okay. He didn't even drive me home himself. He clearly isn't interested. But, oh man, am I.

Just thinking about Hadrian makes me feel alive, hot, wet.

I take another step on the plank. Right foot. Then left foot. My steps are slow but sure.

There's something out there in the darkness. Something on the other side that is calling to me. It's making promises of heat, pledges of delight, vows of bliss.

Hadrian?

No. It can't be him. It's my mind playing tricks on me. But, hell, deal me in on this game.

My feet move on their own accord. Behind me, I hear cheering. I ignore Tate. He's likely too high to even understand what's going on. I want to get away from him and closer to that dark temptation. I feel certain Hadrian is on the other side.

I am not thinking of my dad any longer. It's Hadrian I want to turn to. Hadrian's words I want to hear. Hadrian's touch I want to feel.

There is a flash from above. Something whizzes by my left ear. It is too large to be a bug or a bird.

When I turn to look, I lose my footing. I don't have one of those balancing sticks like Philippe the Frenchman. But I am attached to a safety harness. With the help of the straps, I gain my balance back.

I turn and look over my shoulder. I haven't gone that far. Should I turn back?

No. I am determined to go across. Or even stay

put. Any way that I can to keep the sensations coursing through my blood.

My ears perk as someone calls my name. It isn't my dad's voice I hear. The words are intelligible.

There is another flash. This time on my right side. A gust of wind hits me in the chest. Both my feet come off the plank. I am suspended in the air by the safety harness.

The harness yanks, jerking me in its safety straps. There is a moment of silence. Tate's shouts fill the air, but I ignore him. There is nothing he can do.

It's the parachute all over again. Only this time, I do not want to fall. I am dangling by a thread.

Looking down I can see the street. The asphalt is as black as night, not the green gradation of a vineyard. The path is clear. There is no tall man standing below to catch me.

I sway in the air. My body moves like a pendulum swinging between life and death.

I reach up trying to grab the straps. Then my ears fill with the most horrific sound. The sound of the strap ripping.

I am falling.

Tate's screams died moments ago. He is no longer on the rooftop. He's likely fled the scene. Man, do I know how to pick my friends.

The wind is all I hear as I fall fast. The blood rushes inside me from my brain to my heart. From my heart to my toes.

I have no chute to save me. Nothing in reserve. For the second time in forty-eight hours, I am falling to certain death.

And then there are arms around me. I am being pulled out of thin air. I blink my eyes open and he is there.

15

Hadrian

I run all the way here. For the first time in my second life, I am out of breath. The scarce amount of blood running through my veins boils. It goes straight to my head.

I smell her before I see her. Her scent is that of an overripe berry in the wind. She is all around me, swirling over my head, wafting into my nostrils. I look up and my stomach drops.

When I see her walking in the sky, I want to roar. When she slips on the thin beam, I do.

As fast as I am, I will never make it to her in time. She dangles on nothing but a bit of twine. If it were my handiwork and I had suspended her, I know that the binds would hold.

Praise the Fates, the harness she's in does hold.

Those stooges will have a slower death for providing the safety mechanism that buys her time. But I am still going to rake them over hot coals for suggesting the idea to her. Though I suppose I'm the one who suggested it.

The fact of the matter is that they facilitated it.

The reality of the situation is that she did it.

So she is the one who I will focus my punishments on.

Yes, that is my plan. As soon as I get my hands on her, I'll turn her ass red. I'll make her pussy weep. I'll make her lips quiver as she begs for my mercy. And I will show her none.

She wants danger? She wants to feel. Oh, she's about to feel something, all right.

As I plan which of my instruments to dust off from my old collection, the harness that holds her safety snaps. She is falling again. Falling fast. Too fast this time.

She doesn't fall straight. The wind pushes her dangerously close to the brick of the building. If she impacts it, her flesh will rip, her bones will break.

There is no parachute floating over her to

break her fall. If she lands in my arms at that increased speed something in her fragile body will fracture. I cannot have that. Not before I have the chance to break her body, her mind, her will into submission.

I blur, faster than any vampire has ever moved. Dust mites become visible. The cricket's sharp notes elongate. Hydrogen molecules collide to form air.

I scale the building, digging my nails into the brick and grabbing footholds until I am to her. Just in time is an understatement. I grab her body to me and throw us, my back first, into a window.

Shards shatter and clatter down onto the cold, hard floor. The sharp points pierce my skin and instantly heal. The only blood I smell is my own... for now.

I have her. She is cradled on my chest as I lie on a bed of glass. I hold her for long moments. Just listening to the sound of her ragged breath.

When her breathing slows to match mine, I rise. She is still cradled in my arms. There is no way I'm putting her down. I move to a corner of the office space away from the glass.

Her eyes open slowly. She looks at me, her eyes filling with wonder, disbelief, and then tears.

"Do you have a death wish?" I bellow.

Her lips part. "What?" She gulps, trying to take in more air. "No. I-"

"You nearly died. If I had been one second later you would've met the sun."

Her head shakes, eyes opening and closing as though she's trying to focus in the dark room. "The sun? What are you talking about?"

"Of all the idiotic, ill-conceived, monumentally stupid things to do."

Her face contorts. Pain and hurt are etchings in the grooves around her eyes. "Let me go."

"No."

I know I hurt her feelings with the name calling. Better I hurt her feelings than the street break her back. She struggles to move, but she cannot. Once again, she is bound in a harness and served up on a platter to a practiced sadist.

"You've shown me you can't be in charge of your own life." I latch my hands around the harness straps and tug her chest to me. Her lips are only an inch away from mine.

"Where in the hell do you get off?" she shouts.

There is fire in her cinnamon-colored eyes. The heat of them wakes up something deep inside. I can smell the blood pumping through her. She is angry and her essence will be spicy.

"I saved your life," I say. My bottom lip brushes her mouth as I speak. "Not once but twice. It's mine now."

"What?"

Carignan's gaze is wide and aroused. Her blood is nearing the right temperature for me to gulp her down. I plan to take a healthy gulp of her. Soon.

"I'm coming to collect," I say.

I let go of the strap. Her body tumbles back. I catch her head before it can hit the ground. Then I am over her.

"What are you ahhh-" She gasps. Sucking in air through her wide-open mouth. A keening sound comes from somewhere deep in her chest as I pull the strap of the harness, the one that touches her right thigh.

With my nail, I rip through the tough fabric of the strap. Keeping the pressure, I move the edge of the strap along her inner thigh until it runs right up against her right labia. The fabric of her jumper is no hindrance. I could make out the outline of her pussy with my eyes closed. All I'd need is my nose to know the parameters of her desire.

"You say you don't want to die?" I ask.

"No," she whimpers. "I don't. I just want to feel."

"To feel what?" Inching the edge of the strap in

the space between the crease of her inner thigh and her pussy, I press inward.

Carignan takes a deep breath before she is able to speak. "Like this. The way I feel when I'm with you."

The room is dark. A sliver of moonlight casts a small ray of illumination. But I see her perfectly. When her wine-colored eyes latch onto mine, I know she can see me too.

Taking the other half of the cut strap, I knot the two pieces back together. Her right leg is now splayed wide. The edge of the strap I've wedged between her thigh and pussy digs into that space. Not touching where I know she needs it to, it's a constant tease of a release only I can give her.

She whimpers again and reaches her hand to me. I catch her wrists in one of my hands. Breaking off another bit of loose rope, I twine her hands together and stretch her arms over her head. I tie that end of the rope to the desk's leg.

She is stretched out for me. Arms pulled tight. One leg splayed open for me. Time to get to work.

I snap the strap holding her left thigh. Her leg trembles in its freedom. Using the edge of the strap, I press it flat over her core.

Carignan bucks off the ground. But she can only

lift her hips, and only an inch or two off the ground. She is almost entirely at my mercy.

There will be no relief unless I give it. There will be no escape unless I offer it. And I am not feeling charitable.

"Hadrian," she whispers in the dark.

I barely hear her. My gaze is trained on the nectar between her legs. I've only rubbed the strap once and she has soaked the fabric of her clothing. She is so wet that the imprint of her labia is clear.

I press deeper. Turning the rope to the sharp edge so that her core is divided in half. I do this lightly. She strains towards the ropes, towards me.

"Do the ropes get you off?" I ask.

"Yes," she moans. "Yes, please."

I'm so used to my victims taking time before they beg. Not Carignan. I don't even need to ask her to beg. She does it so readily, so prettily.

"Do you want more?" I ask.

"Please," she begs. "I want more. Please."

She is not the only one who is wet. My mouth is so filled with desire that I can't swallow it down fast enough. My fangs are dripping with a need I haven't had in centuries.

I wipe the top of the strap over her clit. Back and

forth like a windshield wiper would. Like my tongue soon will.

Her hips chase the motion. She is unpracticed. Has no man ever taken his pleasure from that bud? No man but me ever will.

No man but me will ever see her like this. Hands bound and stretched. Thighs spread. Hips trembling. What I wouldn't give for a flogger to watch her body jerk and jump.

I know her nipples must be tight pebbles. Her eyes flutter closed. Her mewled words become unintelligible.

I have her total surrender. If she were in confession, she would tell me everything, give me anything. All I want is her release.

Her body's natural pleasure-seeking brain has taken over. I know this because her hips move in tight circles. Her chest heaves in short pants. Her eyes blast open as her orgasm takes her.

Her fingers twitch. Her eyelashes flutter. Her belly quakes. All while she screams.

It's then that I can take no more of the torture that I am inflicting. I pull the strap taut over her quivering pussy, and I take her lips. My kiss is as brutal as her orgasm. It's a jerking, rocking, biting thing.

One fang sinks into her plump lip. A bead of her sweet blood seeps out. They say it only takes one hit of heroin to become hooked.

It takes one drop of Carignan, and I am addicted.

She is still bound as she comes down from her orgasm and I return to my senses. But the ropes mean nothing. She is mine. And I am keeping her.

I snap the remaining ropes of the harness with my nail, tearing the frayed edges into a sharp edge. She is quiet, docile, sated. I feel like I just awoke from a long slumber.

I glance down and that's when I notice it. The edge of the strap that is attached to her harness, half of it is frayed. The other half is a perfect edge. As though it has been cut with a straight edge.

The taste of her blood on my tongue goes bitter. Her fall was no accident. Someone cut the harness.

16

Cari

I've diddled my pleasure bump before like any curious girl who wanted to understand her body. There have been a few tingles, a pleasant rush, even some thigh squeezing as tiny ripples of pleasure tickled my toes. But there has never been waves wracking over my body, pulling me under so that I can't breathe. I have never been pulled under, water going over my head, my body convulsing as pleasure breaks over my entire being.

My throat is hoarse from begging Hadrian. Begging him to stop. Begging him to not stop.

Begging complete gibberish as my brain turned to mush and my body turned on me.

Once the tremors stop and the world rights itself, I am sure all my fingernails are cracked and broken from clenching them into my palms. I can't feel my pinkie toes because they are so curled. My knees are knocking together now that they are no longer bound. I'll definitely need to call a chiropractor because I'm certain I've thrown my back out.

I stretch my limbs. Though I'm no longer bound, I'm not able to get very far. The harness and ropes are gone. I am in someone's arms. I know it's Hadrian's arms because of the warmth and the feeling of utter safety.

I open my eyes and see the honey gold of his chest. I inhale and the spicy scent of him tickles my nose. I splay my hand over his chest.

Surprisingly my palms are dry of blood. My nails are intact, mostly. I flex my feet and straighten my back. Looking down I see the nail on my right middle finger has bent, but it's hanging on.

There is a warm hum still buzzing through me. Not the strong current of the orgasm. I can still feel, and I feel alive. I am alive. Hadrian has saved me. Again.

We are walking. Not in the building in downtown. We are outside in the moonlight. The scent of saplings fills the air. We're in a vineyard.

How did we get here? Did he drive? I don't remember getting into a car. I don't see a car. Did I sleep the entire way? I guess it's possible. I must've blacked out after the orgasm.

"Hey?" I say.

Hadrian lowers his gaze and regards me. A sliver of moonlight curls around his cheek. "Hey."

I feel each of his ten fingers on me. I know their exact locations. Ten pressure points that are the only thing keeping me tethered to this plane of existence.

I've been running away for a year, diving into thin air, leaping into the unknown. For the first time that I can remember, I don't want to move. I just want to stay put. Forever.

"Are you still angry with me?" I ask.

Hadrian doesn't answer. His gaze roves my face. I feel each place his pupils land, like one of those heat sensors. Though it's my nipples as well as my cheeks and lips that are so hot right now.

"I'm not suicidal," I say, remembering his accusation.

"I believe that," he says. "You like the rush. It's clear to me now."

His gaze slips to my nipples. The twin points are

completely wanton and they perk for him. His nostrils flare like he can tell.

"But you will not be doing any more adventures," he says. "Not without my leave."

"Your leave?" I ask.

"My permission," he clarifies.

A giggle escapes my lips. Then a laugh, followed by a very unladylike snort. My sister raised me a feminist. "Like, what? You're the boss of me now?"

His green eyes are as hard as jade. His lips thin into a cruel line. "That's exactly what it's like."

Something inside me rears up like he spoke a long-held truth.

"I've saved your life twice now," he continues. "You owe me two."

"I..."

I what? Wasn't this what I wanted? To be with Hadrian.

And he knew it. He knew it by the way I acted when he gave me that mind-blowing orgasm. It blew me away, so hard I blacked out.

"You're mine now."

That is crazy talk. I could've jumped out of his arms. His hold is loose. But I hold still.

A delicious heat washes over me from my fingertips down to my toes. It pulses in my core. A stronger pulse than my first skydive. Steeper than the first step onto the plank. Faster than my first time around the race track. I feel it is only the beginning.

"Yes," I admit.

"*Ragazza brava.*"

My Italian is rough. But I think he just called me a good girl.

"What are you going to do with me?" I ask, still not struggling in his arms.

"I'm going to punish you."

"Punish me? Why?"

"Because you're mine and you nearly broke my possession."

There's a war raging inside me. Hot and cold. The heat flushes out of my pores with the fact that I am his. But my ardor is cooled by shame remembering my actions earlier this night.

"But didn't you already punish me?" I say. "Back in the building When you... you know?"

"You mean when I fucked you with the strap of your harness and made you come all over your panties?"

I swallow, but the lump stays in my throat. I nod but my head feels light and heavy at the same time.

"Say it." His voice is a hiss, like the devil tempting Eve with forbidden fruit.

I reach for the apple and bite. "Wasn't my punishment being fucked with my harness strap and coming in my panties?"

Saying it out loud doesn't sound like a punishment. It sounds like a gift. And I want another bite of the apple.

"No, *stellia*. I let you come. I'm not going to be so nice this time. I'm going to strip you bare. Tie you down. Bring you to the brink of orgasm over and over again. But never let you crest. Not until you learn your lesson."

I am panting. I am writhing. "My lesson?"

"That the only jump, the only leap, or dive you ever will want to take will be that peak into an orgasm that I bring you to."

He sets me on my feet. For the last ten minutes, he was the only thing in my sight. Now I see that we are in his bedroom. He steps behind me. The door is wide open in front of me. I could run.

I turn to him. His gaze is stern, like an avenging god.

"I'll be good," I say.

I see the pleasure spark in his gaze in real-time.

"But," I say, "There is one thing you should know. I'm a virgin."

17

———

Hadrian

Carignan's declaration doesn't rattle me. For all intents and purposes I, too, am a virgin now. I've been celibate for nearly two centuries. That's over two lifetimes.

But I don't tell her this. I take her by the hand and lead her to my bed.

Unlike Gaius, I actually sleep on the mattress and not hardwood. Being born poor and sleeping on straw for the majority of his life makes it a difficult habit to break. Gaius showcases his riches in his clothes. But when he closes his eyes, he is still the broken slave that he was born, the man who fought hard to win his freedom, only to lose it to a vampire seductress.

Gaius's daytime proclivities are not my concern right now. Carignan and her pleasure are. I sit her down atop my pillow top mattress, another of my favorite modern conveniences. Though my family wasn't poor, straw was the height of comfort in my youth. I'd burn the fodder before I let it come in contact with Carignan's soft flesh.

There's not much else in my bedroom other than the bed. There are clothes in the closet. A few odds and ends I've collected over the centuries are tucked in the closet as well. I'm not very sentimental. All I care for is either planted in the vineyard outside or down the hall preparing to turn in for a day's rest. Grapes and my blooded brothers. Everything else always turns to tatters and fades.

Carignan will fade someday, as well. I will never turn a living soul and condemn them to this existence. At some point, I will have to tell her what I am. She will grow older and watch me remain youthful.

And yes, I plan to keep her that long. Perhaps when she goes to ground I will finally step into the sun. But that is a ways off.

She is here now. Safe. Under my protection. Under my command.

I will find who slit her safety harness. That person I will torture and show no mercy. No one tampers with what is mine.

But first, my little daredevil needs to learn her lesson.

The torn harness is long removed from her skin. Only the jumpsuit and her footwear remain. I cup her calf to remove her boots one by one. The moonlight is at my back as I work. The windows of my private sanctuary are dressed with blackout curtains, my favorite convenience in the advancement of technology. Before I lose my head in the valley between her thighs, I press the button that casts us into complete darkness.

Because I want to look upon my new possession, I rise to light a fire in the hearth. Incandescent bulbs and fluorescent lights would destroy the mood.

Carignan waits for me on the bed. She shivers, but I know it's not from the cold. I take pleasure in making her wait. She knows what I can do to her body with just a strap of fabric. I know she's anticipating my cock.

I peel off the layers of her clothing to reveal sun-kissed flesh. So different from Domitia. She was paler than porcelain. Unlike the fine, ceramic material, Domitia was unbreakable. But she enjoyed having others take a crack at it.

Domitia and I fought for dominance in the bedroom, in life. Carignan gives me her total submission. She acquiesces as I peel the jumper from her breasts. She is pliant when I urge her to lift her hips to rid her body of the garment. She yields as I divest her of the remaining scraps of fabric that cover her intimate places. Perfectly obedient.

"I want you to kiss me," Carignan demands.

I lift an eyebrow as I tower over her. "You're in no position to make demands."

Her chin lowers, along with her eyes. "Please?"

I've never heard that word from Domitia. *Now. Again. Harder. Faster.* Yes, all of those were a regular utterance. But never please.

I capture Carignan's lips with my own. It's like tasting one of those sugar sweets that has a hidden center of something even sweeter. It takes everything in me not to bite down to get at the center of her Tootsie Pop.

I lick at the fleshy part of her lips. I suck at the underside of her tongue. And then I crack. I nick the space at the center of her upper lip.

The essence of Carignan is pure saccharine.

Richer than honey. Denser than the darkest choco-late. The shock of the sweetness goes to my head.

I rear back.

My fangs elongate, dripping with need.

Carignan's eyes are shut. Her neck is exposed. I realize then that she has complete trust and faith in me.

I swallow. My fangs retract. For now.

Wrapping my hands around her hips, I lift her and toss her body back towards the headboard. She startles and flails.

Good. She needs that jolt to wake up. To be alert. There is a monster in the bed.

"Hands," I growl.

It takes her a second, but she offers me her hands. I take the edge of the expensive sheet and I tear. With the strip of fabric, I bind her wrists. The loops of the sheets make the sign of the cross as I fasten her hands together. There is no savior in this room tonight.

Her gaze goes wide. Her breathing goes shallow. Her tongue darts out and she licks her lower lip.

The sound of fabric ripping again snaps her back to attention. She bites down on her lip as I bind her breasts. Again, I make the sign of the cross, making sure to leave her nipples exposed for my torture.

Carignan offers not a single whimper of protest. She holds still as I strap her body down and manacle her hands to the headboard of my bed. I sit back on my haunches to admire my handiwork. I only look for a second before I am on her.

Her lower body arches off the bed when my tongue attacks her left breast. I lick and suckle. She writhes and shivers. By the Fates, she might be one of the rare birds who can come from nipple stimulation only. But we will test that theory later.

I slap the edge of the bind across her breast and she snaps out of the trance. Her lips pout like a child whose toy has been taken away. She is not getting the point of all this.

"Please, Hadrian. Tell me what you want."

"*Sei una ragazza brava.*"

I tear another strip of the sheets. Stretching down the length of her body, I bend her leg at the knee. The knot I tie here is tight. It leaves her core exposed to me, as it always should be. I can't wait to hogtie her, but that will be for another night.

"Please, Hadrian. I need you inside me."

"*Sei una ragazza brava.*"

After tying her other thigh so that she is both exposed and immobile, I come down slowly to my belly. I simply gaze at her weeping pussy. Those tears are all for me. No sharing. Just mine.

I take my first taste.

Carignan can't move. She can only feel. That's what she said she wanted. That's exactly what I'm giving her.

I lift her ass in my hands and bring her to my mouth. I taste each of her folds singly. Fuck if she's not sweeter than a mango. I swirl my tongue over her pink flesh, tugging her labia with my lips all the way to the edge. At the edge of her intimate skin, I break the skin.

Sweet blood and cunt juice. Fuck me. I meant to torture her with pleasure. But the pain of not having my dick buried deep inside of her is becoming too much to bear.

Her whimpered pleas weaken my will. The taste of her on my tongue clouds my resolve. The feel of her, alive and trembling in my hands, makes me forget my purpose.

I know where she wants me. Her pussy pulses with need, leaking more tears. I slap her inner thigh, to bring us both back down. Carignan screams her frustration. Now she's getting it.

"Sei una ragazza brava."

My dick is weeping now. I give her another knick

on her right labia, taking in another sip of her blood. Her punishment is nearing an end because I can't last much longer. My hips buck into the mattress as I suck her clit. Her bud is overripe, begging to be plucked.

"I am," she whispers. "I am being a good girl."

Thank the Fates she figures it out. Too bad I can't answer. My mouth is full.

Her hips rock only slightly in the binds, but her pussy clenches hard around my tongue as her inner muscles convulse. As I spill into the sheets, I lose all semblance of control. My fangs sharpen and I sink my teeth into the crease of her thigh.

I swallow her down into my throat, into my heart, into my soul.

She is a part of me now.

She is mine.

But the real lesson that we learned this night, is that I am hers.

18

Cari

I am an early bird. Have been my whole life. But my eyes simply refuse to open to the new day.

I have a lot of false starts. Waking and dozing. Something demands that I rest, that I stay put.

It is no hardship. My body feels heavy from pleasure. Oh, the pleasure I experienced before falling to sleep. Part of me wonders if it was a dream. But I know it was real.

There is an ache between my thighs from being forced to stay open. There's also an irritation down there, right at the crease of my thigh. I supposed the binds Hadrian used chafed there.

But I'm not bound any longer. I am free. My fingers and toes are still curled from clenching hard. And long. And repeatedly. I didn't know multiple orgasms were a thing. I thought that most women don't even experience orgasm their first time.

Wait? Was that actually my first time? Hadrian didn't penetrate me with his penis. So, technically I am still a virgin.

A very satisfied virgin. A very satisfied virgin who does not want to get out of bed. But I want to see what this new day with Hadrian has in store for me.

My thighs aren't open any longer. I can press them together. But when I do, the space between my thighs, my intimate lips feel swollen. I'd rather keep my legs apart.

My knees are no longer bent so I stretch them to the edge of the bed. I stretch my arms out too. Reaching my limbs down and out to the sides of the bed I realize I have the entire queen bed to myself. I am alone.

Hadrian cut me loose from the binds. And he left me. My eyes have no problem springing open with that devastating realization.

And there he is.

He sits by the bed in a tall backed chair. His chin

rests on one hand. His thumb rubs his bottom lip. His gaze is intent on me, watching me.

"There you are," I say.

"Where else would I be?"

He doesn't move to gather me to him. Or kiss me. Or return to the bed. He simply looks at me.

I am covered, but naked beneath the sheets. Somehow I feel the sheets are no barrier for him. He sees all of me. He always has. Even from that first night... way back two days ago.

"You always show up exactly when I need you," I say.

He tugs at his bottom lip. Pressing the plump flesh between thumb and forefinger. I note that there is a tattoo on his bare chest. It looks familiar, like something I'd seen in a history book at school. A crest with a cross in the center. A sword on one side and a tree branch on the other.

I fidget with the edge of the bedclothes, staring at his chest instead of meeting his gaze. "Why is that?"

"Fate," he says.

I shift in the bed. I don't want to get into a discussion of God and how He's let me down. No. That wasn't why I asked Hadrian that particular question. That wasn't what I wanted to know.

"How?" I ask. "How is it that you're always there exactly when I need you?"

I sit up. The sheet falls away exposing my breasts. Hadrian's gaze latches on to my girls. My nipples greet him with a full-pebbled salute.

I pull the sheet up. Not out of embarrassment. He's seen me from angles I haven't seen myself. I just want his full attention to answer my question.

Hadrian's gaze lifts from the sheet to my eyes. And holds. And holds.

After a second too long, I get the message. I let the sheet drop as per his silent command. Then I move the sheet from my torso as well, giving Hadrian a view of all of me. All that he owns.

He said it last night. But this morning I come face to face with the truth of it. I am completely owned by this man; body and soul. And my heart is fast catching up in the transfer of goods.

"*Ragazza brava.*"

Hadrian rises from the chair and looms over me. I'm certain he doesn't stand over me to prove his dominance when he sinks to his knees. With the barest of nudges, he parts my thighs and puts himself between them.

"The answer to your question, *stellia*, is very

simple. But you are not ready to hear it. I will tell you when you are."

I don't question him. I trust him. He opens his palm and I give him my hand, just as I'd done with my life.

Hadrian kisses my knuckles. Then my fingertips. The numbness of the past year has been gone since yesterday. It was like I was alive again.

"I want to talk to you about something else." He pulls my body onto his, cradling me against his chest. "Would anyone have any reason to harm you?"

I nuzzle into his chest. "Harm me?"

"Do you have any enemies?"

I rest my hand on his heart. "Enemies?"

No, I'm not really listening. I'm fascinated by the warmth of him, the smell of him, the feel of him.

Hadrian puts his forefinger under my chin and lifts my head. I obey, giving him my undivided attention. He lifts a brow, clearly not appreciating my parroting. I think back over what he's said to me.

Harm me? Enemies?

"I'm sorry," I say. "But the question is just ridiculous."

The idea is laughable. So I do. I laugh.

Hadrian does not laugh. He looks very serious.

"I don't have any enemies," I say. "Why are you asking me this?"

He reaches to the nightstand. I don't see what he has until he holds up a strap. At first, I think he's ready to tie me up again. My entire body coils in anticipation. But it's a harness strap, not a rope or a torn bedsheet.

"This was cut," he says, running his finger over the top of the thick fabric.

I look closer. It's the harness strap I'd worn last night on the plank walk. "This is from when you saved me? When you cut me loose."

"No. This happened before. Someone cut it before you stepped on the plank. And then it tore. What happened was no accident. I'm starting to wonder if the first fall was also an attempt."

"An attempt? An attempt at what?"

His gaze latches onto mine and holds. I know his answer. But it's ridiculous.

"Carignan, is there anyone that would benefit from your death?"

My lips set to say no. But something stops them. I look into his clear green eyes and I wrack my brain for the answer he seeks.

"My brother and sister. Marechal needs me to agree to keep the vineyard open. But Arneis wants me to agree to sell. I'm the deciding vote. They're waiting on me to make up my mind."

The words tumble out of me without stopping. I shudder at the force with which they are wrenched from a dark place inside me. Hadrian gathers me to him. His heat ushers away the cold, dark feeling.

"I'm sorry," he breathes into my hair. "I needed to know."

I push him away. I'm not sure why, but I feel violated. "My siblings would never do anything to hurt me. No one's trying to kill me. Those were accidents. What I was doing was dangerous, not a walk in the park."

"Okay," he soothes, bringing me back to him.

I come back into his arms without protest. I don't think I could ever deny this man anything.

"Okay, *stellia*. They were accidents. Accidents that will never happen again. I've got you."

He folds me in his arms and I let him. We stay like that for long moments. The room is dark. The fire has died down to embers.

"I should probably head home," I say. "What time is it?"

"Six o'clock."

"In the morning?"

"At night."

I jerk out of his hold, looking around for a time-piece. "I slept the entire day?"

"I was thorough with your lesson," he says, prowling toward me. "And I'm not done with you."

"I... my brother and sister, they'll be worried. I'm supposed to have dinner with them tonight. In an hour."

Hadrian's jaw turns to stone. I think he's about to forbid me to go. Yeah, that is definite disapproval on his brow. I know it well from the way my siblings look at me after each adventure.

Before Hadrian opens his mouth, something shifts in his features. "Fine," he says. "But I'm taking you."

19

Hadrian

I sense Carignan's reluctance at the command in my voice when I tell her I'll be coming to dinner with her. I do not temper my tone. I do not ask for an invitation to the family dinner.

I do realize that dinner with the family after only two days of knowing each other is fast. I don't care. This was a full-blown relationship the moment she fell into my arms. Her safety is my highest priority. She said so herself that her siblings had reason to harm her. I will cut their ties to her if I scent a whiff of ill will coming off of either of them.

"I need to go home and get dressed." She grabs her destroyed jumper from the other night.

"There are clothes for you here," I say as I walk through a door to an adjoining closet.

Carignan follows. Her feet are bare. A sheet is wrapped around her naked form. I do not bother with clothing for myself. I'd much prefer to keep her nude and in the bed. But I can make time for this little outing.

She gasps as I open the closet doors to reveal a full woman's wardrobe. There is a department store hanging on the dressers and inside the drawers.

"You dress a lot of women the morning after?" she asks.

"These were all purchased specifically for you."

"For me? When?"

"While you slept. I had them ordered and brought in."

I put in a call to the three shifters just before the sun came up. I never had any intention of taking her to her home. I have no intention of letting her out of my sight again. Until I reveal who and what I truly am, keeping her asleep through the day will be diffi-cult. But not so much.

She is highly susceptible to my wishes. Each

time she woke in the day, I only needed to nudge her mind to send her back to sleep.

"Pretentious," she says as she fingers the sundresses.

I smile, eager to have her model each one for me. But not as much as I want to decorate her skin with twine and bind her to the mattress.

"I guess you do this a lot?" she says after selecting a deep purple dress that brings out the cinnamon color in her eyes. "Seduce a woman to your bed and have everything she needs the next day. Cute trick."

Her head disappears inside the dress as she pulls it over her head. When her face pops out I am the first thing she sees. She swallows at the displeasure on my face.

"There's never been another woman in that bed," I say.

Her lips part. Her fingers fumble on the ties of the dress. I take over while I watch her features shift and contort, trying to figure out the puzzle of my words.

"Well, you haven't been here very long," she says.

"No. But I intend to stay for a very long time." I pull the last tie tight, gathering her to my chest. "And I plan to keep you with me."

Her features relax, no longer shifting to decipher my meaning. My words are pretty clear. I think she's finally getting the picture.

"Man, you slept late. I've been waiting for you — oh!"

We both turn at the unwelcome interruption of Gaius' voice. He is lucky she is dressed. Otherwise, I'd have to gouge my best friend's eyes out.

Gaius stands in the doorway and simply stares. His lips move and nothing comes out. The male is never at a loss for words.

"Carignan, this is my brother Gaius. Gaius, this is my... Carignan."

"Yours?" asks Gaius. "So soon? But I suppose I shouldn't be surprised. You fell hard for-"

I clear my throat. If Carignan weren't pressed against me I'd flash my fangs and tear into my brother's throat. Luckily, Gaius gets the hint and recovers.

"*Enchante, mademoiselle.*" He takes Carignan's hand and bows over it like the courtly noble he pretends to be.

"*Tout le plaisir est pour moi, monsieur,*" she says in perfect French.

"Carignan's family owns Durand," I offer, mostly to keep that baby talk language off her tongue.

While they chat, I take the moment to slip on clothing of my own.

"I've sampled the white wine," says Gaius. "It's very good."

He's lying. He hates white wine. I don't bother to call him on it. I'm too busy wincing as Viri walks by the door in a kilt and cowboy boots.

He stops and stares at Carignan. From here I can see his fangs.

"Since when do we order take out?"

"She's not here for dinner, Viri," says Gaius.

"A prostitute then?"

"She's Hadrian's special friend."

There isn't much that scares vampires. We are the highest predators on the food chain. Even more deadly than lion shifters.

Viri's face goes ashen. A visible sweat breaks out on his forehead. He steps back from the doorway. His hand cups his privates. "Is she going to bind my dick in chains? I hated it when Domitia did that."

"Viri, manners," said Gaius.

Instead, Viri dashes out of the doorway and down the hall. His heavy footsteps boom as he makes a run for it. He was a favorite toy of Domitia's, but he did not appreciate her attention.

"Viri is not good with people," Gaius offers.

"Carignan, would you mind if I borrow your Latin Lover to talk business for a moment?"

"We're headed out," I say, navigating myself and Carignan around Gaius. Grapes are the furthest thing from my mind.

"It's important," says Gaius. "We're experiencing a bit of root rot with the grapes. It's spreading along the vines. Nothing I'm doing works. Look."

Gaius holds up a sickly vine. There isn't much I can do. My father's vineyard never experienced root rot. Any vineyard in the Middle Ages that did was in danger of losing it all.

"I've seen that before," says Carignan. "My sister would know how to treat it. We're headed over there now."

My head jerks to Gaius. I glare at him. Like an annoying sibling, he ignores me and invites himself where he is not wanted.

"Wonderful," says Gaius. "I'll join you."

I place Carignan in the back seat. Gaius takes the passenger seat with the wilting vine in his lap. The drive is relatively short to the Durand vineyard.

Gaius and Carignan keep up a conversation over berries and vines and growing up on a vineyard. Something Gaius didn't do until he had a century under his belt. My thoughts are on the siblings.

Could one of them have cut that harness? I watched many blood relatives turn on one another during the Inquisition. I was only ever sure of the truly guilty party when I compelled them to talk. Often both had a bit of culpability.

Not my Carignan. She is guileless. I'd know even if I hadn't compelled her.

I do feel a modicum of guilt over that. I only did it to get the truth out of her. I would never do it to influence her feelings for me. Those I know are real.

I never had that before in my life. Domitia had initially compelled me to want her. But she hadn't had to push hard. After our first fuck, I was in love. I was also young. Very young.

Would I have felt the same had I had more experience? I don't know. It doesn't matter.

We arrive at the Durand estates. The house is a sprawling one story. We pull up around the back where the winery is.

Gaius beats me to the back to let Carignan out. He smirks as he takes her on his arm. He's playing with fire and he knows it. But he does not want Carignan. He never wanted Domitia. He just likes to get under my skin, the asshole.

The storefront of the winery is closed to the public this late in the evening. Carignan opens the door and steps across the threshold. Gaius and I halt in the entryway.

"Are you sure it's all right that we come inside?" I ask.

"Of course it's fine," says Cari. She doesn't glance back at us to see that we have stalled in the doorway.

"We don't want to disturb your sister's work," I hedge.

Carignan turns back. Her eyes narrow. Her head cocks to the side as she beholds the two of us standing in the doorway.

I hate that she is beyond my grasp. She can't see it, but my body is pressing against the seal of the entryway, impatient to get back to her side.

"Don't be silly," she says finally. She raises her hand and waves us in. "Come on in. I want you to meet her."

I exhale as I step across the threshold. I am on her in a second. My hand is around her waist pulling her body back to mine. Behind me I hear Gaius chuckle as he falls into step with us.

We venture deep inside, to a laboratory. A woman dressed in a tight-fitting skirt beneath a lab coat is bent over a set of vials. Beside me, I see Gaius lick his fangs.

"Marechal?" Cari calls. But the woman doesn't lift her gaze. Cari tries again, louder this town. "Mare, I'm sorry I'm late."

Marechal looks up, startled. Her dark brown gaze is so like Carignan's. "Late? Oh. For dinner. I'm so sorry. I forgot. I'll just finish this up really quick." She pauses, finally noticing me and Gaius. "You brought guests?"

"That's Gaius Serrano and this is —."

"Oh, the Serranos. You purchased the old Palmezzo Vineyard. You should know that soil is prone to root rot."

"So we've learned." Gaius holds up the affected root.

"A classic case," says Mare. "I have just the cure."

"Mare," says Carignan. "Before you start the shop talk, I'd like you to meet Hadrian."

"And Hadrian is?" asks Mare.

"Hadrian is my..."

"I believe the proper term is boyfriend," I say.

Mare frowns at me. "Boyfriend?" She turns to Carignan. "Since when do you have a boyfriend?"

"Since... now," says Carignan.

Mare gives her full attention to me. Her shrewd gaze narrows as she looks at me over her glasses.

"Your family label has been around for quite some time. You inherited the business?"

"I started working as soon as I could walk," I say.

"Me too," she says. "I take my family business--all of it--seriously."

"You seem a serious woman. The kind who'd do anything to protect your bottom line."

Marechal squints over her glasses. It's her gaze that latches onto mine. She stares directly into my eyes, as if she is the one that's probing me.

Her will is strong. But I have her in my grasp. I search her mind and come up with formulas and mixtures and a deep abiding love for Carignan.

Marechal blinks a few times after I release her. She glares at me as she pulls open the side of her white lab coat. Within her coat are a pair of cutting shears.

"If you hurt my sister, you should know that I carry sharp things in my back pocket."

Beside me, Gaius chuckles. I can tell his interest is piqued. I nod at Marechal, liking her even more myself.

"I mean your sister no harm," I say. "Her care and protection are my highest priority."

After a moment, Marechal nods. She shuts her lab coat. "I believe you."

"And I believe you."

20

——————

Cari

"Where'd you find him?" asks Mare.

"When I was out skydiving."

Her intake of breath is sharp. So is the glare she turns on me.

What? It was an honest answer. And I was never one to lie to authority figures like teachers, my dad, or my older siblings. Though it was easy getting away with things when Mare was in charge of me. She was usually up to her arms in soil with her head in the vines. I'm not used to her giving me her full attention as she's doing now.

"Another adventure junkie?" asks Mare. "What's he into? Racing? Volcano jumping?"

My head tilts to the side as I regard my sister. Of course I told her about all of my adventures. But she was analyzing grape hybrids as I did so. So, I'm shocked to the core when she can rattle off some of the crazy stunts I've pulled.

"No," I say. "Hadrian's not into any of that."

There's an unsaid question mark at the end of my statement. Because I'm not exactly sure if Hadrian is into adrenaline sports or not. He had given me the idea for plank walking. But had he done it? Is that how he knew?

It hits me then. I really don't know much about Hadrian, my lover, my boyfriend. The man I'm ready to give my virginity to without a second thought. The man I let do wicked things to me that I had never even known were options in the bedroom.

What I do know is how he makes me feel; safe and secure. It just goes to show that sometimes it pays to take a risk.

However, I'm not feeling the itch to jump out of a plane tonight. Or to walk between high-rises in the morning. Nope. There is a new itch. This itch is lower in my body and more centralized. I want Hadrian to take me back to his bed and –

"It's that serious?" Mare's eyebrows are raised so high they form golden arches near her hairline.

She's staring at me. I have her full attention. Probably for the first time in years.

She gasps, but in an exaggerated way that ends in a grin. "He's plucked your berry."

"Mare!"

In the distance, I see Hadrian's head lift. His gaze finds mine. It's like he's in tune with my every move. I feel his bright green eyes roam over me in the darkness. I am heated just by his look.

I have two pairs of eyes on me, his and Mare's. Luckily, Hadrian is too far away to hear this embarrassing conversation.

"We're sisters," says Mare. "We can talk about these things. Especially since you grew up without *Maman*. I should've sat you down earlier and had this talk."

"We are not having this talk." I can feel the flush creeping across my cheeks and I turn away from my sister.

Like any parental figure who wants to both embarrass their charge and at the same time educate them, Mare goes on as though she didn't hear me, or is just ignoring me. "You had that health class in school. I remember I signed the permission slip for it."

Mare was over eighteen when I was in high school, so our father allowed her to behave like a guardian when it came to school and after school activities. It was great on some levels. I got to go on coed camping trips and even a study abroad where the students far outnumbered the chaperones. But there were drawbacks to having your twenty-year-old, data-minded sister as your guardian.

"You had cable hooked up in your room with all the channels," Mare is saying. "And the internet. I assumed you'd figure it out."

I put my head in my hands. For someone who makes fine wine, Mare has no filter. She will talk about skinning grapes in the same conversation as the mating rituals of fruit flies and then over to the nitrogen content in manure. No, she was not adopted. I asked.

I chance a peek between my fingers. Hadrian's gaze is still locked on me. And he's grinning like he knows what we are talking about. I assume it's because he can see my red cheeks from the distance...and under the moonlight?

"But I suppose there's a lot of misinformation on

the internet," Mare continues. "Especially on the porn sites."

I can hear Hadrian's chuckle from where I sit. Not only is he great at catching me when I fall, but he can also hear over long distances when I'm being embarrassed, too? My head goes back into my hands. Mare is oblivious, so she keeps up the sex education.

"Orgasms are not normal for women. Multiple orgasms are a fantasy written in bad porn scripts. In fact, seventy-five percent of all women never reach an orgasm during intercourse. Many never reach one in their lifetime."

Huh? That's not my first experience or my second with Hadrian. I must be one of the rare anomalies then. I'd had multiple orgasms without intercourse.

Now both Hadrian and Gaius are looking this way. Though Gaius is focused on Mare. His dark brows are lifted as he regards my sister, as though antlers are growing out of her head.

"I just don't want you to be disappointed when the time comes," Mare is saying. "Hadrian seems to care about you."

The pink washes from my cheeks as I turn back to her and speak my truth. "I trust him with my life."

I want to make her understand how important this man is to me, what his simple touch has done for me. "He makes me feel alive again."

Mare's hand comes to my low back. It's a comforting weight. Her touch travels up my back and settles in my heart, like a warm blanket.

"I know this last year has been hard on you with...everything," she says. "Cari, I want you to know that, if you decide you don't want anything to do with this place anymore, if it's too painful to be here and you want to sell, I'll understand."

Looking at my sister now, a memory from when I was young rises to the forefront of my mind. I remember her holding my hand when I learned to ride a bike. I remember her arms around me, hugging me when our mom died. I remember her lips pressed to my forehead, telling me everything was going to be all right, that she was there for me.

"It's not your fault that he's gone, Cari."

"I know."

Mare brushes a tear from the corner of my eye. "He would've wanted you to live, to walk away from that accident. He would've done anything for you to survive."

"I know. He said so before he died."

I have never told anyone that before. Not either

of my siblings. Not the therapist who tried to help me deal.

"He told me to get out of the car and live," I confess. "I've been walking around like the living dead for months. I've been so numb. The adventures, the adrenaline, it was the only way I felt alive."

Mare runs her hand over my brow and down my back. Her touch sparked old memories of summer picnics out in the vineyard, cold winter nights watching Christmas movies under a wool blanket.

"And now?" she asks.

I look up at the night sky. I haven't seen the sun for two days but it feels like a new dawn.

My gaze lands on Hadrian as he walks to me. My heart races, my blood pulses, my breath quickens. All with my feet planted on the ground and my body sitting still.

"He brought me back to life."

21

Hadrian

I scoop Cari into my arms. Lifting her up and out of the lawn chair. The glass of wine she holds spills. It is one of her sister's special hybrids, a good bottle. But I do not care.

I brought her back to life, she said. She has no idea what those words do to me. What they mean to me.

For the first time in my second life, I feel no pain. I feel no shame. Death does not taunt me. Cari's arms around me, her smiling face, they outshine my memory of standing in sunlight. It's as though I can feel the sun's rays and they warm me instead of burning me.

Is this what Cari feels? Is this what it is to feel alive? I had forgotten. But holding her in my arms, the memories are coming back.

I put my nose in her hair, burrowing into the side of her neck. Her vein pulses as though it knows its new master. The jugular punches me in the mouth, taunting me to take a sip of her sweet nectar.

Oh Fates, how I want this woman. How I need her. In my mouth. On my cock. In my very veins.

But I can wait. We have time. We have her whole life.

I trace my lips from her throat to the underside of her chin before I take her lips. She is sweet heat, salty sass, and spicy strength in one serving. And she is all mine. Wrapping my hand around her neck, I tilt her back to take more.

From the side of my shoulder, I hear a rumble. The sound does not detract me from my mission of consuming Carignan. The disruption sounds again, deeper this time, insistent.

It's Gaius clearing his throat.

I tear my mouth away from Carignan and flash my fangs. I will not share her. Best friend or not. Blood brother or not, I will rip his *petite* head from his body before I let him put his dainty hands on her.

Instead of challenging me for Carignan, Gaius raises his brow. He tilts his head and nudges it to the side a couple of times. It's like he's trying to tell me something in an unspoken language.

From my peripheral vision, I see what he's trying to say. I'd forgotten we have an audience. Marechal, the sister. Luckily, she is sitting on the other side of me so she doesn't see my fangs.

I retract my teeth, take a deep breath, and set Cari down. But I do not let her go. I will never let her go.

"We can have dinner another night, Cari," says Marechal. "I see you're a bit... preoccupied at the moment."

Carignan is dazed. Her gaze is hazy and unfocused. Pride wells up inside of me. I did that to her.

The simplest things about her bring me the greatest amount of pleasure. Her honesty. Her vulnerability. Her clear and tangible desire for me, and only me.

"If you're not too busy," Gaius turns to Marechal, "I'd love to preoccupy you."

"I beg your pardon?" Marechal peers at Gaius over her glass and her glasses.

I can't tell if she caught Gaius' sexual intent or not. He's been sneaking covetous glances at her since we arrived. When she began her ridiculous talk of the myth of the female orgasm, I knew that all that Gaius heard was a gauntlet being thrown down.

He'll have her in his bed before the sun comes up, of that, I have no delusion. Most women drop their panties at the quirk of Gaius's brow. But looking again at Marechal and her studious gaze, I can see sexual satisfaction is not the direction her mind headed towards.

"Oh, you mean you'd like to talk about your little problem with your tool."

Gaius' smirk drops. "My what?"

"The tools you'll need to fight root rot. I'm sure that like me, you can easily get wrapped up in vines."

Gaius makes a choked sound. Carignan's cheeks heat. Even my little innocent gets the double entendre. Her sister remains oblivious.

"I didn't realize we were having guests for dinner?"

The new arrival looks familiar to me. But I can't place him. Not until he takes a stiff step towards me, his lips curling in distaste, his Chianti-brown eyes flashing in disapproval. Then I remember where I know him from.

"Hey, Arneis." Cari goes over to the man and embraces him. "I want you to meet my boyfriend. Hadrian, this is my brother."

The recognition is now a two-way street. We bumped into each other at Club Toxic. Frangelico had taunted the man when I was on my way out of Club Toxic. Though there's knowledge in his gaze, he doesn't make our connection plain.

"Boyfriend?" says Arneis. His lips curl.

I've never had to do the parent or sibling thing. Domitia was half a millennium old when she turned me, and many of her sireds were long gone, by her own hand. I knew growling and baring my teeth was not the way to go in this meet and greet. I have no idea what to do otherwise.

"Hadrian and Gaius own the vineyard a few miles away," says Marechal.

Arneis does not look impressed. "You're in the wine business? Upstarts?"

"My family has had vineyards for hundreds of years," I say, knowing that the Durand vineyard is less than one hundred years old.

Arneis' brow quirks, but only slightly. "If you're looking to buy this place, and trying to get a leg up by dating my sister, you can cut ties. I already have a buyer lined up."

"Arneis," says Cari. "What a horrible thing to say. Papa would be ashamed."

Cari's older brother grits his teeth. His glare remains on me and not his little sister. I don't catch a spark of shame in his dark brown eyes. He doesn't look directly at me.

Does he know of the paranormal world? Is he clued into vampires and what we can do? It's against the rules. But Frangelico is king here, so he can break the rules if he wants.

"You should know I've decided I don't want to sell," says Cari. "This place is a part of me. It's a part of Papa. I don't want to let it go."

Arneis turns from me now. He whips around to face Carignan. "Don't be rash, Carignan."

I am beside her, ready to knock this pompous ass into the middle of the vineyard if he dares bring any aggression on her. But by the looks of it, I will not have to.

Carignan puts her hands on her hips and faces off against her brother who has a couple of inches on her. "Don't be rude, Arneis. I know my own mind. I'm not a child."

"You've been behaving like one all year," he says.

And then his features soften. He brings his hands to her shoulders. "You're not well enough to make this decision. I think you need help."

"Help?" Marechal steps up to the other side of Carignan. She puts her hand on Carignan's hip and tugs her younger sister towards her. "What are you talking about, Arneis?"

"She needs psychiatric help, Marechal. We can't deny it anymore. The skydiving, the racing, and now this." His hand waves in my direction. "She's making reckless choices. We should commit her."

"Touch her and I don't care what blood runs through your fingers, I will break each one just above the knuckle."

Arneis takes a step back at my threat. Marechal looks between the two of us. She's clearly upset with her brother, but my words give her pause. Gaius is at my back. I'm not sure if he's there to aid or stop me. All I care about is Carignan. She places herself between me and her brother.

But she faces me.

Her hands rest on my chest. If she tells me to back down, I will. For now.

"I want what's best for her," Arneis says after a tense silence.

"You're looking at him," I say.

Once again, Arneis' lips curl. Once again, he does not look impressed. "We'll see about that. This isn't over."

Arneis looks to Carignan, then to Marechal. Before he goes, he gazes out at the vineyard, as though it is another family member that turned on him.

"I need a drink," says Marechal after her brother storms off.

"Pour me one, too," says Gaius.

I pull Carignan into my arms. I run my hands up and down her back, trying to infuse warmth into her after that scene.

"He's not usually like that," says Cari.

I don't care. If Arneis thinks he can take her away from me by medical hold or a snip of a harness, he is mistaken. I will happily rip him limb from limb. I'd make it look like an accident, of course.

22

———————

Cari

"Where are we going?" I ask from the passenger seat.

Hadrian shifts through the gears of the sports car like he's slicing through a piece of cake. He takes the turns with one hand while the other moves from the gear stick to my knee and back again. I want him to stick to a steady speed, or even slow down, whatever it will take for him to keep his hands on me.

Gaius stayed behind to talk vine health with Marechal. I don't think they'll end up in bed. Though I got a decent helping of Mare's full attention tonight, I'm certain that was the top portion of her daily quota of consideration away from her work.

Arneis stormed off after that awful display. I have no idea what got into him. Or the measuring contest that got underway between him and Hadrian.

Well, maybe I do. A mental institution? Really? My brother already sent me to a therapist and I followed her prescription.

Okay, not to the letter. But her advice worked. I am back in a car right now.

Hadrian speeds through the streets. My heart races as he takes a hairpin turn with only one hand on the steering wheel. I want to ask him to slow down. But my voice is in my throat. I click on the seat belt and hold onto the edge of my seat.

"We're just going to make a quick stop in Tucson," he says, answering the question I forgot I'd even asked. "Then I'll take you home."

He removes his hand from my knee. Instead of reaching for the gear shift, he reaches up and brushes his knuckles down my cheek. My fingers unclench from the seat. My body warms with only the slightest touch from him.

"I'm sorry about Arneis."

"Don't mention it again," Hadrian says.

But I have to. "It was just the shock of it all. My decision to keep the business. And you're my first boyfriend."

"Your first?" He takes his eyes off the road to glance at me.

"Only."

He grins as he takes another turn, his green gaze makes me feel like a priceless gem. "We're going to keep it that way."

This relationship between us should not be moving this fast. We've only just met two nights ago. But there are many cases of love at first sight. Tons of movies and books about it. I wonder if this is love that I'm feeling as we do eighty miles per hour in a forty zone.

"You don't think we're going too fast?" I voice my concern.

Hadrian removes his hand from my face and places it back on the wheel. The speedometer on the dash ticks down as he engages the brake.

"No," I say. "I mean us. What's between us. It's happening so fast. I mean, we barely know each other."

We're in the heart of the city of Tucson. I recognize a few of the buildings around us by the high rises in the skyline, but I haven't been to this particular street before. He's parked in front of a club. The people walking in and out look dazed as though they drank too much and won't remember the good time they had inside.

Hadrian reaches over. He unstraps me from my belt. He lifts me up out of the passenger seat and brings me into the driver's seat with him.

After settling me in his lap, he asks, "What do you want to know?"

I look into his eyes. They are clear, open books. I know nothing about this man. But what I do know is that I have access to everything inside him.

His every thought. His every wish. I need but ask. He would give me his all.

So why am I holding back?

"I just want to know one thing," I say. "One thing that you want me to know about you."

Hadrian opens his mouth. Then closes it. He swallows hard. After a moment he places my hand on his heart. "I want you to know that it's never felt like this for me before."

The warmth from his chest seeps from his flesh and into my fingertips. Something pulses in the palm of my hand. Then it arrows straight to my heart.

"You've been in lo-." I cough to cover my flub. "I mean you've had other lovers before? Of course, you had other lovers."

Hadrian unfurls my fingers from his chest and brings my palm to his lips. "Only one."

That arrow in my heart twists. But not painfully. He's turned a lock and the floodgates rush open. My eyeballs go to my hairline and I see my skull.

But I temper my response. He did say one. There had been someone else before me.

"Domitia?" I repeat the name I'd heard earlier tonight.

Of all that's happened between us in the last forty-eight hours, it's those four syllables that make Hadrian wince. What had Viri said she'd done to him? Put his private parts in a vice? I wonder what he meant by that metaphor?

"You loved her?" I ask.

"I...?"

I hear the question in that single letter. His gaze clouds. He squints, looking off into the night. Finally, Hadrian sighs and rests his forehead on my chest. I cradle his head like he is a child in need of comfort.

"Where is she?" I ask.

"Dead." He takes a deep breath and lets it out before he continues. "I never thought I'd feel... anything again. And then you fell into my arms."

Hadrian lifts his head from my chest. My hand still cups his face. He rests all of the weight of his worries and cares there.

"Fast or slow," he says, "I don't care about the speed. All I know is I want to feel this way forever."

"Me too," I agree.

His kiss is slow. His lips take their time on the curve around my lower lip. As they reach the bend of my top lip, the speed and the urgency increases. Neither of us pumps the brakes as we crash into one another. Our mouths are on a high-speed chase that just might end in our total destruction.

He kisses my forehead tenderly when he pulls away. Then my eyelids. Followed by my nose. He shifts in his seat. I note he wasn't wearing his seat-belt, but I don't comment.

"Do you want me to wait in the car?" I ask when he reaches for the door handle.

"No." He opens the car door and steps out with me in his arms. "We won't be inside for long. But stick close to me."

"Is this place dangerous?"

"Your life will never be in danger with me."

Hadrian places me on the ground and takes my hand. Our fingers twine as we walk to the closed doors of the club. The sign overhead reads Club Toxic. I don't think I've ever heard of this place. When the doors open and my mouth gapes, I see why.

23

Hadrian

I keep my hold on Carignan tight as we leave the writhing bodies of the top floor and descend into the dungeon. The first time I came through these doors, the deviant acts and depraved inhibitions had no effect on me. But when Cari hesitates on the threshold and presses her ass back into my groin, I get an immediate rise.

I wrap my arms around her. Partly for her protection. Mostly as a display of my possession of her. It's paramount that every man, monster, and beast in this room recognize upfront that this woman has been claimed.

She hasn't even entered the room and her scent already has a few nostrils flaring. I catch the eye of a tall, wiry vampire. My vision is sharp, so I see the glint of fang. I flash mine fully, hissing a low warning. The vampire lowers his gaze and moves on.

Carignan's fingers tremble as they search for mine. She entwines her hands with mine and squeezes. I squeeze back to reassure her. But as her scent wafts up to my nose, I'm not sure that it's fear that I'm scenting on her.

I take in the dungeon through her eyes. The naked woman strapped to the Saint Andrew's Cross moaning in pleasure as a man flogs her bare cunt. A row of men and women bent over spanking benches as canes play a drum roll upon their asses. In the open play area, two males hold a woman in between them as they double penetrate her ass and pussy, pumping in and out in time to the music. The woman's head lolls back and from side to side in ecstasy. I'm not entirely sure she's still conscious.

Cari squeezes my hand again and presses further back into my chest. I hold her to me, assuring her that no one will touch her.

That's why I brought her in with me. The hell would I leave her in the car on the street. My suspicions of her brother aside, wolves and vampires roam these parts freely. The safest place for her will always be by my side, in my arms.

"This is a sex club," she says.

"Yes."

"Are you... into this?"

Is it my imagination? Is it wishful thinking? Or do I note a hitch of interest in her voice?

I have every intention of training her in the ways of the erotic arts. Or what is known today as BDSM. But in private.

Having her arms wrapped around me earlier and her fingers entwined with mine now is a new kind of joy. But I ache to tie her down, have her entirely immobile while I pleasure her to unconsciousness so that when she wakes from her orgasmic stupor there will be no doubt in her world that she is mine.

For now, I follow her gaze. It is on the woman tied to a Saint Andrew's Cross.

"Does that interest you?" I whisper in her ear. The tip of my tongue touches the cone of her ear and I taste the heat that has spread from her cheeks to her ears.

Her head tilts back. Her gaze flicks to me. Then down to the ground.

Perfectly submissive.

"I..." She bites her lower lip as she sneaks another glance. "I don't know."

Lies. She will get a punishment for not speaking her true desires.

"Maybe," her gaze lifts. Her fingers twist, pulling and tugging at the skin around my knuckles. "But not with an audience. I don't want to be passed around or for others to see me like that."

I spin her around to face me. My grip on her shoulders is a bit rough, but I need her to understand this most important fact in her new life. "You belong to me."

Her gaze hoods, as though her lids have grown heavy with desire. Her chest lifts as she takes in a deep breath. The outline of her taut nipples is clear beneath the fabric of her dress. Praise the Fates she does not resist my claim because she no longer has a choice in the matter.

"No one else will ever taste what's between your thighs or in your veins."

"My veins?" Her fog of desire clears momentarily.

I have no idea how long I can hold my tongue about what I am from her. I already know that I can't hold my fangs at bay. A pang of desperate hunger is growing inside me. Blood bags simply will not do any longer. At least Viri will be happy.

"Why, if it isn't the Prince of Pain, himself."

I look over Carignan's shoulder to find Frangelico approach. The Vampire King is not alone. His queen is with him tonight.

I've heard of the wolf who claimed Frangelico's heart and drank his blood. She is a beauty. White blonde hair, long limbs, and a feral look in her eyes that warn that she isn't entirely tame.

"Such manners," purrs Frangelico. "You've brought a fresh toy to play with? A delicacy at that. She smells untouched."

"She's mine," I growl, tucking Carignan behind me.

"Understood." Frangelico smiles, clearly unfazed by my show of dominance.

I am in his house. Surrounded by his sireds. Besides that, Frangelico is ancient. He wouldn't need help disposing of me. But I need his help. So I take a deep breath and try to focus.

"She will not be touched without your express permission," says Frangelico. "You're welcome to stay and play as long as you like."

"We're not here to play," I say. "I need information."

"The man who wanted no part in our politics has come to me two nights in a row to ask a favor?" Frangelico turns to his bride who has not taken her gaze off me. "Selene, will you take Hadrian's guest to the bar for a drink while we talk?"

Kissing Cari's knuckles, I relinquish my hold on her and hand her to Selene. Carignan's gaze is questioning. I can only nod my head, hoping she will trust me. She does and turns to go with Selene.

Selene is a newly made vampire. But she is also a wolf. She has a modicum of my trust. But I still track their movements and don't take my eyes off Cari.

"What can I do for you this time?" asks Frangelico.

"Arneis Durand. What is he to you?"

"Well, seeing as you're here with his baby sister, I feel I should be asking you that."

"He was here two nights ago. Why?"

"A bribe." Frangelico shrugs.

My teeth clench until my molars grind. If Frangelico had anything to do with Cari's near-deaths, I don't care how many of his sireds I will have to gut, I will start a war.

"A zoning issue I paid to have swept under the table," he continues. "Standard political swamp.

Arneis Durand likes to pretend he's above it all. And for a time he was. But now he's cash poor."

"Cash poor, you say?"

"Durand Vineyard has fallen on hard times since the father's death. But the enterprise is still quite lucrative. Arneis wants to sell to pay off debts, but the older sister is tenacious. I've made a very generous offer."

"The Durand Vineyard is not for sale any longer."

"Really?" Frangelico raises a brow.

"Really," I insist.

Frangelico shrugs again. I'm certain it's no skin off his back. The vampire is richer than a Saudi prince. "As long as my personal cellar is stocked, we won't have any problems."

I let out the breath I'd been holding. This was not exactly a dead end into who sabotaged Cari's safety harness. Arneis has motive. I need to get the man alone, where I can force him to look me in the eye and tell me the truth. But that will have to wait.

"My offer stands to stay and play," says Frangelico.

My gaze has not left Cari. Her back is to me. I have a clear view of the outline of her ass. My mind is outlining all the things I want to do with it.

Yes, I think we will stay to play.

24

Cari

The door snicks closed behind us. I stand in darkness. A second later there is light but only enough to see what's before me.

On a small platform is a large apparatus that looks like a giant tripod. At the center of the three legs of the contraption hangs a metal hoop. I try to take in a deep breath, but my lungs are too busy pushing air out as I pant.

What have I gotten myself into?

Hadrian walks around the tripod and begins checking its knobs and gears. His face is all business as he does so. Complete focus and concentration, like he's done this before.

Of course, he has. He tied me up expertly last night. I watch him now as he takes varying lengths of rope.

"The Prince of Pain. Why do they call you that?" I ask, partly to distract myself from what I've agreed to. Do I really even know what I've agreed to?

"It's my old job," he says as he inspects the rope, running his fingers along the twined strands.

I'm not sure what he's looking for. It all looks like it's unbreakable to me.

"Which was?" I prompt him when he does not elaborate.

Hadrian's gaze flicks to mine. "I used to hurt people, Carignan. Does that scare you?"

"So you were mafia?"

"No. Worse. But not anymore. Not for a long time." He places the rope aside but doesn't come to me. "Aren't you going to ask?"

"Ask what?"

"If I will hurt you?"

"No." I shake my head with certainty. "I know you would never."

The look he gives me is inscrutable. But I know

I've said the right thing. It was an easy answer. It's the truth.

Although I'm nervous about what's about to happen, I have not a single doubt in my mind that Hadrian would never hurt me. I might feel a bit of pain. But the times he's bound me the pain was fleeting. The pleasure was exquisite. I'm happy to go through a bit of agony now that I know what's on the other side.

Hadrian holds his hand out to me. I go to him without hesitation.

"Don't we need a safe word?" I ask.

He grins down at me. He dips his head down and kisses my nose before turning me around. I feel his fingers in my hair, gathering my strands and tugging at them as he weaves my hair into a braid.

"No safe word. I know you. I know how you respond to me. I know what you need. Better than you do, it would appear. Just tell me what you need and I'll give it to you."

Well, that's easy. "I need you."

"I know," he says as he lets me go.

The long braid falls and taps between my shoulder blades. With fast, sure fingers, he peels the dress from my body, followed by my underwear. I'm naked before him and I've never felt so free. Hadrian takes a place beside the tripod.

"Stand here, Cari."

His voice is full of command. It sends a shiver down my spine. I go where he instructs me to go beneath the tripod.

He picks up a length of rope and walks toward me. I stare at the rope and my breath catches in my throat. Any tension releases from my body on a strained exhale as my nipples tighten to hard points.

"Is this what you want?" he asks.

I look from Hadrian then back to the rope. He stands before me; tall and gorgeous, eyes intent on my body as he charts a path to my pleasure. My skin prickles as the air conditioning kicks on from above blowing at the fine hairs on my forearms.

My ears perk up. My eyes are so focused. It is sensation overload.

"Yes," I whisper.

"Hands."

My hands come up on their own accord and I present my wrists.

"*Ragazza brava.*"

He takes my wrists in his hands. His touch is electric. He guides my hands behind my back, folding one forearm over the other. His chest presses into my back, his hips and torso meet my ass. His belt buckle brushes against the skin of my lower back.

He wraps the rope around my wrist. The feel of the ropes and their restriction ignite something within me. I am at his mercy, the mercy of his sure hands.

Hadrian rests his chin in the crook of my neck as he pulls the ropes taut. My head lolls back to rest against his cheek. I tilt my head up, offering him my lips.

"Spread those pretty thighs for me, *stellia*."

I open my legs, a little off balance since my hands are tied behind my back.

"*Ragazza brava*."

He kneels behind me. I hear a cap flip open. Then I feel fingers on my pussy lips. I gasp, almost teetering over from my wide-legged stance. But Hadrian lends me his chest for balance. The fingers on my pussy lips are warm and wet. He rubs lube on my clit and labia, slowly, lightly, until I am panting. With just that light touch, I am close to orgasm. Hadrian pulls his fingers away from me as soon as I start to tremble.

I hear the cap open again. Then I feel the same wet warmth on my anus.

Wait? What? But I don't have time to reject his touch at my exit.

He circles my puckered hole a few times before he enters. My eyes flutter at the sensation as he pushes his finger in. I gasp again as he pushes in knuckle-deep.

With his finger up my ass, it takes a moment for my mind to work. Is he about to take my anal virginity before penetrating me vaginally?

But he withdraws his finger. I clench at the vacancy. My eyes open as he rounds me. He places a pink anal plug on the stand before us. Hadrian examines the plug and then regards me.

Does he want my permission? I can't open my mouth to form words. I'm not sure what I'd say if he asks. Do I want something up my ass? I'd never even considered it before just a moment ago.

Hadrian walks behind me with the pink plug. A second later, I feel the cool plastic of the pink plug greet my anus.

"Bear down," he says.

I do as I'm told. The plug slides home without any obstruction. Hadrian gives it a firm push. I feel the end of the round suction stopper on my ass cheeks. The plug isn't painful, but neither is it pleasant. There is a slight discomfort, as though my body knows it shouldn't be there.

Hadrian pulls my chest back, forcing me to stand up straight. The plug changes angles and a feeling of fullness takes over in my body, leaving me feeling invaded. The fullness is delicious, and it spreads throughout my body.

"Do not come," Hadrian commands. "If you come now it will be the only time I allow it. Do you understand?"

No, no I don't. "Yes." I squeak.

"Just wait for it, Cari," he whispers in my ear. "It'll be big and beautiful, I promise."

Hadrian comes back to stand before me. There is rope in his hands. He wraps the rope around my waist, his thumb and forefinger brushing over my flesh. I am so hypersensitive that I sense the difference in temperature of his fingernails as he threads the ropes, and then the pads of his fingers as he pulls the rope taut against my skin.

He walks around me as I stand on display for him. Hadrian's touch makes my nipples hard, but his gaze pierces them into fine points. His breath against my abdomen makes my pussy slick. And then there is the plug.

It's too much sensation. I have to shut my eyes.

But the loss of one of my senses does not de-tune me. Desire is a fuming cloud in the air that invades my lungs with every inhale.

And then there is the touch of the ropes. The thread Hadrian uses is silky and coarse at the same time. It moves like satin on my skin as he makes his loops. Every time I make the slightest movement against the grain, I meet with a delicious friction. I have to fight to keep still and not squirm for the sheer pleasure of it.

Hadrian ends the first bit of knot work with an intricate large node that rests on my belly button. The weight of it sparks desire in my gut, and that desire sinks lower into my throbbing, wet pussy. I am on fire and soaked at the same time.

Next, Hadrian passes the ropes between my legs. I nearly buckle over as the dry rope hits my slick wetness. He keeps me upright as he pulls the ropes up the crack of my ass like a g-string. With his fingers, he arranges the ropes at my pussy on either side of my clit. The ropes that hit my crack push the butt plug another millimeter inside of me.

My lips are trembling at this point. There is a tremor in my hands as I try to hold still as he continues. This is the sweetest agony I've ever experienced in my life.

Somehow I have the presence of mind to remember Hadrian's warning. He told me that if I came without his permission it would be the only time I came tonight. I grit my teeth, ball my hands into fists, and try to rein in the increasing pleasure.

Hadrian continues the knot work behind me until another heavy knot rests at the base of my spine. Each tug of his ropes brushes against the bind at my pussy. The ropes squeeze around my clitoris. My legs are shaking. When I begin panting, Hadrian stops. He comes around the front and stares at me. He doesn't need to use his words to warn me not to come.

"I didn't," I say. "But I really, really want to."

Hadrian's all-business veneer cracks a smile. "You're being a very good girl, Cari. I'm very pleased with you. I just might let you come sooner than I'd planned."

My body sags in relief, but the moment I let go of my hold I feel an orgasm knock on the door. I grit my teeth and press my heels into the floor. Hadrian waits a moment, watching me. His expression tells me he expects me to fail at this moment, to come against his command. Hell, I expect me to fail at this moment.

But I don't. I get a hold of myself before my inner

muscles clench. I raise my chin at him in triumph. Hadrian smirks, but I can tell he is impressed.

He reaches the rope over my head and loops it on to the ring of the human-sized tripod. He gives the rope a tug, and I am airborne.

The ropes take all of my weight and leave me without a care in the world. They cradle me in the twine, leaving me with nothing to hold on to. There is nothing holding me back. I am restrained, but I am flying. I am free. This is pure bliss.

Hadrian gives me a gentle shove, and I am truly flying. As the slight breeze hits me in the face the ropes press against my pussy, giving me a rough friction. On the way back, I feel the pressure in my ass. It pushes the plug even deeper.

There is nothing I can do now. There is no floor to ground myself into. I clench my hands, but it isn't enough. An orgasm is coming soon whether I want it to or not, and Hadrian is nowhere near finished toying with me.

Next, he wraps a chain around my breast. The cold metal is a shock to my system. It brings my attention from the heat between my thighs on my pussy and ass. My mind reels between the cold chain, the friction of the rope, and the heat both materials create. And then there is Hadrian, whose hands continue to tug at the ropes and run against my skin.

I am wrapped up in all of these sensations when a buzzing sound starts. I open my eyes to see a Magic Wand in Hadrian's hands. Just the disturbance of the air caused by the motor of the vibrator sends shivers down my spine.

Hadrian runs the vibrator all along my body, over spots I'd never considered to be sensitive. He rests the vibrator on my nipple, already a tight rock. The chains rattle over my skin causing the sensations to multiply tenfold.

I pant. I beg. I plead.

Almost instantly I am rewarded when he runs the vibrator over my pussy. It doesn't come in direct contact with my labia because there are ropes in the way. Hadrian puts the wand on the ropes. The vibrations go through the ropes and directly to my clit. My hips jerk making the ropes seesaw against my front and back openings.

Hadrian takes the vibrator away. "You want it?"

"Yes! Yes, Hadrian, yes."

"Beg me."

"Whaa?"

He turns the vibrator off and crosses his arms.

"Please, Hadrian. Please let me come."

With a cocky grin, he turns the vibrator back on. Just the sound has me jumping out of my skin.

"Please, Hadrian. Please." It becomes a chant. "Please, please, please. Please, please, please."

Finally, he puts the vibrator back on my thigh. The closer it gets to my core, the more my body tenses in anticipation. My stomach flutters. My panting diaphragm causes the ropes to rub against my skin.

My heart pounds. I am breathless. I tingle all over.

Finally, Hadrian waves his Magic Wand over my happy place.

I look up at him, pleading, delirious.

He gives me the slightest of nods.

Sparks fly like in a magician's spell. It's like my body is liquid and the vibrator is an electric cord. I lose control of my limbs as they jerk in each direction in response to my clenching inner muscles.

The orgasm starts on my clit but then travels down the rope to my labia. As I clench internally, the butt plug dings pleasure sensors I never knew existed, which then zip back down to my labia and back up to my clit.

The cycle repeats on loop until I black out.

25

Hadrian

I should stop. I know this, but I can't bring myself to. Cari is breathtaking when she orgasms.

Her nipples strain like a berry so ripe it's ready to fall off the vine with no aid. Her belly trembles in wave-like ripples. Her round ass clenches molding to perfect globes. But it's her lips I can't take my eyes or my mouth off.

She makes the most perfect sounds. Most of the time it's my name she says. But she softens all the consonants until they're close to vowels.

I want to hear her say it over and over again, so I keep the vibrator pressed to her clit as the pleasure wracks her body. The moment one orgasm begins to crest, I move the wand to her ass in search of a deeper anal orgasm. When her back bends, I press the wand into her pussy, angling the device towards her g-spot to keep the sweet agony rolling through her.

She begs me. To stop? To continue? Her words aren't exactly intelligible.

The only reason that I do relent and move the wand from her is that I ache to have her in my arms. When the buzzing of the vibrator stops, her pants and moans permeate the room. I lift her from the suspension apparatus.

Her body comes to me with no protest, no push back. She is limp as I cut the bonds that bind her perfect body. But even as I cut each tie, I feel her winding her way around my limbs, my heart, and if I still have it, my soul.

I had always thought love was pain. That it should hurt.

Pain was the body's response to stimulus. The sensation, the ache, the strain; it was the only thing Domitia gave to me. So I determined it must be love.

How wrong I was.

Cari wraps her arms around my neck. Her nails curl into the fabric of my shirt. Her nose burrows into my neck. Her eyelashes flutter closed on my cheek.

She trusts me completely. She has given me her complete surrender. I could do with her whatever I want and she would allow it.

Her feet, though they dangle over my lap, would not run away to another or kick out at me when annoyed. Her hands would not ball into fists when upset and strike me when in a rage.

She sits docile in my lap. With her arms around me. She doesn't see that just as I have her and will never let her go, her hold on me is absolute.

I am nearly at a loss as to how to receive her affection when kindness, tenderness, and care were so sparsely given to me in my entire lifetime.

Any time after laying with Domitia, I was left with a hollow feeling. I originally thought it was because she'd taken my soul. I always felt the need to be filled, and only she could fill it.

Not now.

Sitting with Cari in my arms, brushing strands of her hair away from her lovely face, cradling her bare, lush ass over my straining erection, I feel so full that my fingers tingle. My tongue swells in my mouth, leaving me unable to speak. My chest expands, yet I find that there is more space within the cavity to give her more.

Is this love?

I don't care what it's called. I will fight to keep hold of this feeling. I will die if anything gets between myself and this sensation.

Carignan's eyelids flutter open. "Hey?"

"Hey."

"Are you ever going to actually fuck me? Like, in my vagina with your cock?"

I laugh. Then I throw back my head and bellow. Laughter is a familiar sound. But in my past, it was often preceded by cruelty.

The sound that leaves me doesn't have a trace of pain. I don't cower or wince at it. Neither does Carignan. Joy is a strange sensation. It will take some time for me to get used to it.

"Yes, my treasure. I will fuck you in your vagina with my cock. I will fuck you so hard and so thoroughly that night will become day. But not here. I don't want them to hear the screams."

"Am I that loud?" she asks.

"I will be that loud."

I am going to shout my devotion to this creature from the top of my lungs the moment my cock breaches her virginal skin. I will lay myself bare for her. When I do, the act will make me vulnerable. I might have a modicum of trust for Frangelico now that he's given me aid not once, but twice. But I'd never let any other paranormal, save my brothers, be close to me when I am so vulnerable.

There is a knock at the door. I barely contain my hiss as I glare at the wood of the door frame. My fangs break through my gums, but I don't flash them. I don't want to scare Carignan. I don't know what she'll think when she finds out the monster I really am.

I yank a sheet from the supplies stored in a cabinet and wrap it around Cari. I know that no one would dare interrupt me. Save Frangelico.

When I crack open the door, I see that I am right.

"We have a problem," he says. "An informant in the police force called to warn me that we're about to be raided."

"Raided? But you said –"

"Apparently my politician friend that we spoke of earlier has broken our agreement."

Frangelico doesn't peer into the room to look at Carignan, but I catch his meaning. Arneis has betrayed him.

"Prepare your friend," he says. "There is a back way out."

Before Frangelico can shut the door, I hold out my palm to him. Frangelico stares at my open gesture a second before clasping his palm with mine. I may not have wanted him as an ally, but at this moment I am grateful that he looked out for me and mine.

He did not have to come to warn me. He could have let me get caught up in the raid. Especially if it would mean Arneis' sister might make the head-lines; that would've been a convenient bit of payback for Arneis going back on the bribe he'd instituted.

But Frangelico came to me personally. He must truly have no ill will towards me despite his history with Domitia. I'm not yet ready to call him friend. But I suppose I can no longer call him my enemy.

"Looks like you're in a predicament," says Frangelico. "I don't envy you Sunday dinner with the family."

I shut the door and dress Cari quickly, ignoring her queries of what the matter is. I'll wait until she's out of harm's way to tell her that her brother isn't the man she believes him to be.

Carignan's legs are wobbly, so I carry her out of the room and through the back door Frangelico indicates. From my peripheral view, I see that all of the vampires are moving out of the dungeon. Only the humans are left behind.

I strap Cari into the passenger seat of my car. After I get in on the driver's side, I fire up the ignition. We take off just as the first siren wails onto the street.

"What just happened?" she asks.

"Just a little betrayal. Nothing for you to worry about."

I speed away from the scene. Pushing the car to its top speed, I ignore the traffic lights and signs. My need to get her back to my home trumps all. The sun will be up in a few hours and I want her safely tucked in before the first rays of dawn break.

The headlights that come out of nowhere remind me of the sun. For a moment, I am startled. One moment is all it takes for the crash to catch me off guard.

The tree comes out of nowhere. Then its limbs are everywhere. Through the front end of the car. Through the front of my chest.

26

———

Cari

For as long as I live, I will never forget the sound of the crash that killed my father.

First, there was laughter. His. My Papa wasn't an overweight man, but he had a big-bellied laugh like a mall Santa. But his laugh went hehehe instead of hohoho.

He'd been laughing at me that night. I'd told a joke. I can't remember exactly what I said. I blocked that part out long ago. I only remember the sound of his laugh.

Hehehe. Deep, and resonant. He always closed his eyes when he laughed. I've always known that fact about him. I should've remembered it that night. Maybe if I hadn't made him laugh he wouldn't have shut his eyes. Maybe if he hadn't shut his eyes, he would still be here.

After his laugh, there was a gasp. His intake of breath was sharp and shallow. Probably because he'd been laughing and had exhaled most of his breath.

His eyes had gone wide. So wide, so white that I could make out the lights of the oncoming car in them.

Before I could face forward, I was being thrown back. My father was meticulous about car care, but I distinctly remember the sound of metal on metal, clashing and scraping. The squeal of the brakes was like a record scratch to his laugh track.

Then the squeal of rubber on asphalt. It was like a scream, but not from a human throat. Like the rubber knew what was about to happen. Like it was mourning the loss that it was powerless to stop.

And then came the worst of the sounds. Metal folding into metal.

My father didn't scream. He said two words to me. Then he didn't make another sound. It was my voice that filled the gaps of the metal scraping. It was me that screamed.

Why was this all playing in my head again? Why was it so vivid? Like it was happening again.

I know I'm not back there at the scene of my father's death. I know that I am with Hadrian.

Hadrian. The man that I fell in love with at first sight. The man who I knew, after two nights and countless orgasms, that I wanted to spend the rest of my life with.

Why do I keep blacking out after each time we are together? Will I ever be able to handle his intense loving? Perhaps it just will take practice.

In any case, I don't want to live in the past any longer. I want to move beyond the nightmare that was my father's death. I want to forgive myself because there was nothing that I did wrong.

I'd made my father laugh a million times before that night. He'd only closed his eyes for a second, in the time it took him to blink. There was nothing that I could do to stop it.

It wasn't my fault. I understand that now.

With Hadrian by my side, I have remembered how to live again, how to love. He gives me all the adrenaline I need. It's coursing through my veins now as I open my eyes from the incredible loving he'd given to me inside the club.

I stretch my limbs against the cushion. My arms

and legs are sore. But I expect that after being strung up with ropes and pleasured to within an inch of my life.

I reach for Hadrian. Unlike the last time I woke up in his bed, he is there beside me. I feel his strong arms that held me so tightly the other night. He'd wrapped himself around me and told me nothing would ever hurt me while I was in his care.

So why does something feel wrong now? Why doesn't he reach out and wrap his arms around me? Why does Hadrian feel cold?

I open my eyes and see that we are not in his bed. We are not in the club. We are outside. Under a tree.

How did we get here? I turn to ask Hadrian and my ears fill with screams.

The car has split in two. The tree stands between the headlights. Tree limbs have fallen around us. One large branch is sticking into Hadrian's chest.

No. No. This is not happening to me. Not again.

Hadrian's eyes are closed, but there are crinkles in them. Not like my dad's whose eyes had remained open as I watched them go glassy and lifeless.

Hadrian sighs a long, low sound of pain. He's still alive. And I intend to keep him that way.

I press the buckle on my seatbelt. It loosens and I

fling the strap away from my body. Ignoring the soreness in my legs, I climb over my seat to him.

What do I do? How do I save him? There's a fucking tree limb in his chest.

"Go," he says. "Live."

Karma is a true bitch. Those are the same words my Papa said to me before he died. I do not deserve this. I have been a good girl. I've never hurt anyone.

"You're not dying," I tell him.

Hadrian shuts his eyes as though he's weary. His hands come up to the limb and he tries to grip it.

"You shouldn't move it," I tug his hands away.

"Pull it out," he says.

"You'll bleed out. You'll die."

"I won't. I promise."

It's madness. It's impossible. But I believe him.

"Pull it out," he says.

I take a deep breath. I wrap my hands around the branch. My fingers do not meet at either end. I reach somewhere deep inside myself and I tug the branch.

I tug it like my life depends on it. Because my life does depend on it. If Hadrian dies, I will not go on. I can't. No amount of mental therapy or exposure therapy or adrenaline sports will keep me here in this life.

So, I tug with everything inside of me. Wonder of

wonders, the branch comes free. But with it comes a lot of blood.

Hadrian coughs up blood. It splutters on me, landing on my lips. I know this is bad. Whenever anyone on TV has blood come out of their mouth it always means certain death.

But Hadrian takes a deep breath. He doesn't cough this time. I look down to see the skin around the gaping hole in his chest begin to knit before my eyes.

My limbs begin to shake as I watch the impossibility. Dizziness threatens to take me as I witness the inconceivable. My bladder threatens a mutiny as I crab walk backward and away from him.

"Cari. Cari, stop. You're hurt yourself."

My ass tumbles out of the passenger seat. When I land it's on a cushion of brittle twigs and broken glass from the windshield. There is a pain in my side. I look down and see the red stains on my dress. Through the ripped fabric, I see the gaping gash.

The wound is leaking blood. I feel lightheaded instantly. I'm losing too much blood. And unlike Hadrian, my skin isn't miraculously knitting itself back together.

27

———

Hadrian

The stake only penetrated deep enough to actually hurt. Not enough to end me. It's not the first time I've had something pierce my heart. This was how most arguments with Domitia used to end.

It would begin with shouting--hers. Then pleading--mine. She would screech that I was holding her captive. I would insist that I loved her. But my love was never enough. When I tried to hold onto her she'd go for my heart. She never sent the stake all the way through. She did twist it once when she was really pissed.

If you live long enough, history repeats itself.

But unlike Domitia, Cari pulls the stake from my heart. Cari brings me back to life. Cari makes me want to live.

With the bark gone from my internal organs, my healing has already begun. But I am in a whole other world of hurt.

Cari is wounded. I smell her blood before I see it. My mouth doesn't water at the potent mix of adrenaline and fear that seeps from her body. My fangs are ready to tear apart my own flesh to bandage hers.

The gash at her hip isn't deep enough to kill her. It's deep enough that she will need medical attention, and soon. The elements are not kind to the human body. They break so easily. I know. I am a master of breaking them down.

Out here in the wild, she is susceptible to all manner of infection. Or simply just losing too much blood. But I can heal her. I just need her to stop backing away from me.

"Carignan, stop. You'll hurt yourself."

"What are you? A demon?"

There's fear in her gaze. Her eyes bulge and she stops blinking, as though she's afraid that if she closes them I'll be on her.

I am on her. Not to hurt her. I would sooner

carve out my heart and serve it to her on a platter than allow even her fingernails to break.

But her body trembles beneath me. Tears stain her cheek. Her chin wobbles. Her chest rises and falls in rapid motions.

She is in pain and in panic. Two of my favorite flavors. It makes my stomach turn now.

I want to take it all away. Her fear of me. Her pain. Her dawning knowledge of what I am. I don't want her to find out this way. But here we are.

"I am not a demon," I say. "I am…"

I am what? Because my first statement is a lie.

I am a killer. I am a torturer. I am a parasite. Nothing that any woman could ever truly love.

Carignan blinks rapidly. Her breathing has slowed so that she is taking full, deep breaths. Her body remains tense, but she's no longer backing away from me. She holds still.

"You saved my life," is what I finally say. "Let me save yours."

"Are you even alive?"

"Not before the day that I met you. You brought me back. You made me want to live. You gave me something to live for. I will not let you die now."

I hold out my hand to her. She hesitates. Her gaze flicks over my fingers, my palms. I'd bound her not too long ago with these hands. I'd hoisted her up with my fingers. I'd held her to me with the press of my palms.

Carignan's gaze flicks to my face. I hold her gaze and latch on. I could so easily compel her.

She wants to trust me. She doesn't want to believe that I am a monster. But that is the truth.

I look away from her, no longer able to meet her gaze. I reach down to her hip, where her wound lays exposed. She jumps as I touch her side. But she doesn't pull away from me.

Opening my mouth wide, I let loose my fangs. The sharp points piercing my gums is a familiar pain. Added to that is something new. Cari's sharp intake of breath fills the night's silence. And then she says the word I can not.

"Vampire."

Instead of answering her, I bite my wrist. The blood spills from my veins and over my flesh.

Carignan's breathing is shallow as she watches it, like she is in a trance. I place the stream of blood against her flesh, mingling my blood with her own. Instantly, her blood loss stops. The wound begins to knit itself.

Once her skin is sewn back together, I lift my wrist to her mouth. "Drink," I command.

"You're going to turn me into a vampire?"

"No, my treasure. I just want to be sure you'll heal. Drink."

Still she hesitates. My patience has reached its end. I force command into my voice.

"Carignan, drink."

Her head comes closer. The heat of her breath touches my thumb. Her lips part. And then she pulls back. "Are you mind controlling me?"

"No."

"Have you ever mind controlled me?"

I growl. There's a battle raging inside me. I could press her head to my wrist and make her drink. That would be the most logical if the goal is to keep her healthy and alive.

But I am a man in love. And so I go the irrational, emotional route. "Yes."

Her eyes narrow as she sits up. "You made me do all those things? All those sex things?"

"Did I?" My voice is stony with indignation.

She grits her teeth. Before she turns away, I see the tears. "Did you make me fall in love with you?"

I reach out my other hand. Gently, I take her chin and turn her head back to face me. My features and my voice soften. "Did I?"

Cari meets my gaze. She doesn't answer. But we both know the truth.

Her gaze travels back to my ruined car. The front end is split. The windshield is shattered. Neither of us should have survived. But we have.

Where had that light come from? There is no other car in sight. Had I imagined it? If there was another driver, they left us for dead.

Could that have been Arneis' latest attempt? He clearly knew we were at the club. Could he have had us followed and driven us off the road?

"So you're a vampire?" Carignan hugs her arms around herself.

"Yes." I fight my need to replace her arms with my own.

Her gaze travels over my face, looking at me anew. I hold still under her perusal. But I see nothing change in her eyes. Only a new awareness.

I reach out and cup her cheek. Her arms fall away and she folds her hands in her lap. Her eyes turn to the blood still dripping out of my wrist.

"What happens if I drink that?" she asks. "Will you be able to read my mind? Track me anywhere?"

"I don't need your blood to compel you or to see into your mind."

"So you can see into my mind?"

I nod.

"Well, screw privacy laws then?" She waves her palm in the air as if brushing the notion away.

"Pretty much."

"And the tracking?" she asks.

"I'm only guilty of the normal type of stalking behavior. I would simply follow you to the ends of the earth."

"This is a lot, Hadrian." Her fingers tremble as she rubs at her forehead.

I take her hand in my own, smoothing the skin over her knuckles. "I told you I would tell you when you were ready."

"When would that have been?"

"My original plan was to wait until a decade or so."

Her brows lift as her shoulders cave inward.

"I said forever. I meant it."

"But you can live forever."

I pull her into my lap, making sure to avoid her wound even though it's now healed closed. "I've done forever. All I want in my life is your forever. When you die, I'm coming with you."

"That's seriously next level stalker."

"You say stalking, I say love."

For the last five minutes, Cari had held a mask of

bravery on her face. It crumples now. Her features are naked, defenseless, exposed. "You love me?"

I rest my forehead against hers. "Isn't it obvious?"

Her head turns to my wrist. She takes a deep breath. Then she leans in. When she sticks out her tongue, my dick goes instantly hard.

She tests my blood with the tip of her tongue. Once. Twice. Then she wraps her lips around my wrist and pulls. She had my total devotion before. Now, with my blood on her tongue, I am her eternal slave.

28

———

Cari

My boyfriend is a vampire.

Okay.

I think I am taking it pretty well.

Best thing about having a vampire boyfriend so far? A little car crash can't kill him. So, that's a plus.

And he's a one man emergency room with his magical, healing blood. That'll come in handy for a girl who likes to laugh in the face of danger. Though I'm pretty sure my death-defying days are over.

Between being tied up earlier and crashing later, I'm pretty sure I've met my quota of adventures for life. I'm feeling a bit queasy after this rollercoaster. I want to slow down a bit. Starting now.

"Hadrian, stop. Slow down. I think I'm going to be sick."

We are tracing. For the lay folks that means running at top speeds through the night. The moon's light is all that I can make out as trees and brush whizz past me. Apparently, it's not dark when moving fast. Hadrian's running nowhere near the speed of light, but it's a lot faster than a race car.

Everything is a blur to my eyes. For the girl who likes speed, and heights, and danger, it's not going well with my stomach.

Maybe it was the pint of blood I'd just drank. Or the fact that I'd just been in a car accident. Or the fact that I found out my boyfriend is a fucking vampire.

But I'm playing it cool. Real cool. The picture of cool.

I turn away from Hadrian as I empty the contents of my stomach in his vineyard. Like the best boyfriend ever, he holds my hair back away from my face while I puke.

"I'm sorry," I say when I'm done.

"It's a lot to take in."

Understatement of the century.

Hadrian tugs his ruined shirt over his head and uses it to wipe my mouth. What's not ruined are his washboard abs. Neither are his pecs which flex as he moves. The skin covering his chest is completely healed, though smeared with dried blood. But it certainly doesn't look as though a tree branch was trying to take root.

I thought the tattoo on his chest might be ruined. It's not. It's as though it had never been scratched. Belatedly I wonder how he was able to get a tattoo if he heals so quickly? Maybe he got it done when he was young?

"Can I ask you something inappropriate?" I say. "How old are you?"

Hadrian offers me his hand. When I give him my hand, he tucks my fingers into the crook of his elbow like we're a Victorian couple out for a promenade. We begin walking. I can see his house a quarter of a mile down the road.

"I'm about four hundred years old, give or take a decade."

I stumble, but Hadrian catches me before I fall. "So you're robbing the cradle here?"

"Well," he shrugs, "you are very mature for your age."

"When you said your family's been at the wine business for centuries, you really meant it."

Hadrian scoops me back into his arms and carries me, but he continues at a normal walking pace this time. "I was born on a vineyard. But I had other employment."

"The worse-than-mafia job."

"I worked for the church during the Spanish Inquisition."

"Whoa."

"Whoa, indeed."

"So you, like, tortured people?"

"Not like-tortured. Actual torture."

"And you liked it?" I hedge, trying to determine if my lover was conditioning me for a Red Room of Pain. Though I'm not so sure I am opposed to such a space.

"I was good at it," he says. "It was a way to eat."

I get the sense he didn't take his doubloons out for tapas back in ancient Spain. "You fed from your victims?"

"I did."

Hadrian looks straight ahead. There's a haze inside his green gaze. I can make out shame.

"Well," I say. "That's kinda smart. I mean, they were all bad guys right?"

He doesn't answer. I don't push. No more roller coaster rides for me today. But I am curious about other things.

"How did you become a vampire? Were you born this way?"

"I was turned. By the woman I thought I loved."

His voice is matter of fact, but I sense the hurt in his statement. I know I said no more rides, but what girl can resist knowing more about her guy's ex? Especially when it looks like said guy might bad mouth the ex.

"Domitia?" I hate the way her name tastes on my tongue. "You thought you loved her? You've changed your mind?"

"I have. What I felt for her, what was between us, I know now that that wasn't love."

Hadrian cradles me closer. I tighten the hold I have on his neck as he goes on.

"I thought love was pain. You've shown me just how wrong I was."

It's like I've popped all the balloons at one of those amusement park games with a dagger. Or made all the shots with a basketball at those impossible angles at a carnival. Or guessed the correct number of marbles in a jar at a county fair.

I should quit while I'm ahead. But, seriously?

What girl would when she's getting the dirt on her predecessor?

"You said she was dead. How did she die?"

"We argued. And she walked into the sun."

And now it was game over and I'd struck out. I knew enough vampire lore to know that the sun was a contraindication of their condition. "She committed suicide?"

"She knew it would hurt me."

"That's cold blooded."

"She was. And she was right." The fog has moved from his eyes. They are clear as he regards me. "I've been feeling shame and guilt for two centuries for her actions. But no longer."

My hand slips from his neck to his chest. "I've been feeling shame and guilt for months because of my dad."

"It's not the same. Your father loved you. He would've given his life for yours. Domitia was just spiteful. She was the cause of her own death, not me. You were not the cause of your father's death. Or the accident back there."

My hand falls away from his heart. It comes to rest on my hip where the wound from the crash had been just moments ago. It's healed now.

"Are you going to tell me it was Fate or God?" I say.

"No," Hadrian says. "I won't tell you that."

He walks a bit in silence. I rest quietly in his arms. There's dried blood on his bare chest. My dress is in tatters. We look like we came from a war. And we have.

"So, what do we do now?" I ask.

"I've sent someone to take care of the car. The sun will be up soon. We need to get inside."

"So you can get some rest?"

"No. So that I can fuck you like I promised I would."

"Oh." Should I say no? I'd nearly died back there. But that was my normal everyday life. "Wait? Are you asking me? Or are you making demands?"

"No." Hadrian looks down at me. "I'm begging for it. Please, Cari. Please will you spread your thighs for me. Please let me fill you to the hilt with my cock and give you everything I have until you are trembling and can take no more. And then I'll give you just a bit more. Please."

Well, then. "Sure. Okay."

"Good girl," he purrs.

The rumble in his throat vibrates through me, like the toy he'd used on me earlier that night. Am I even capable of more orgasms? Stupid question. I'm ready to come from just those two words.

"By the Fates," said Gaius. "What happened?"

I hadn't even noticed we'd come into the house. Gaius stands in a silk robe and bare feet, like he's just ready for bed at five in the morning. I note that on his chest is the same tattoo as Hadrian's.

Viri stands barefoot as well. A toga is wrapped around his torso. On his bare chest is the familiar tattoo. In his hand is a blood bag.

"Just a little accident," says Hadrian. "We're fine. We're going to make love now."

"Did she stake you?" asks Viri, his gaze on the dried blood around Hadrian's chest.

"Yes. She did," says Hadrian. "Right in the heart."

29

Hadrian

Vampires take to resting because we can't be out in the sun. Because of the burning and death consequences. Repercussions that no longer interest me.

I peel the tattered dress from Cari's body. There are a few cuts and bruises along her cheek and arms. I bite my tongue. As I kiss each wound I allow drops of my blood to cover her flesh, healing her as I make love to her.

This is my first time making love. For far too long my hands have been instruments of pain. Not tonight. Not ever with her.

I enter her slowly, pausing after each inch I gain into her sweet heat. Cari is eager, greedy to be fully introduced to my cock. I pin her arms down over her head. Though I'll never hurt her, I still need to dominate her.

Her body tenses when I finally give her what she wants. My hips grind into her pelvis. My balls rest against her ass. The fine hairs covering her mons tickle the skin of my lower belly. I own every inch of this woman, yet I want more.

I begin to rock into her. It doesn't take long to realize that I have no hope of lasting long. But that's fine. We have the rest of her life.

I don't sleep a wink after making love with Cari. My body feels more alive than when I actually was alive. I revel in it as I gaze down at her sleeping form.

She says I make her feel warm.

Running my hands over her flesh, my fingertips feel singed. Pulling her back to my chest, my heart burns. Throwing my leg over hers and running my toes over her smooth calves, my loins reignite.

I don't press my need for her. She sleeps like the dead in my arms. I have a moment of panic realizing that one day she will grow old and die.

That's fine. Old age doesn't scare me or turn me

off. I refuse to have her die young. She will live a full life under my watchful eye.

Her human body is so fragile. If her bones break there is no guarantee they'll heal. If her flesh tears, there might be a time when I can't knit it back together.

The thought of losing her turns me cold.

She is mine to protect until she grows old and dies. And when she does, I will go with her. There will truly be nothing left for me here in a world without Carignan.

She stirs and I pull her closer, not liking the few inches her body moves from mine as she stretches her limbs.

"Good morning," she says.

"It's nearing dusk."

The room is cast in darkness from the blackout blinds. There is a small fire burning in the hearth. Because I like to watch the flicker of the flames dance on Cari's skin.

"I slept the day away again. Am I ever going to see the sun with you?"

Not likely. If I can't go out into the sun, neither can she. I need to be by her to protect her at all times. Not only does she attract accidents, she has a proclivity to seek danger out. And there still is that matter of her brother trying to kill her.

"I'm sorry," she says. "Was that insensitive, since you can't, you know? Do you miss it?"

"The sun?"

"Yeah, you haven't seen it in like four hundred years."

I don't tell her that I've fought a losing battle with the sun's rays for two centuries. I don't want her to think I'm crazy. And I don't want to bring up my ex again. Not when I've become reacquainted with joy and happiness for the first time in centuries.

"Do you want to bite me?" she asks.

I give my head a shake. I run my tongue over my fangs. They are not out. "No."

"Oh."

Is that disappointment I hear in her tone? "Do you want me to bite you?"

"I just figured you'd want to, or need to. But I suppose you have those blood bags."

I chuckle as I nuzzle her neck, right over the jugular. "Trust me, a blood bag is no substitute for your taste."

She jerks away. Her hand comes to her neck. "You've bitten me?"

"Only a sip."

She runs her fingers over both sides of her neck and her collarbone and comes up empty. "Where?"

I trace my hand from her breast, over her belly. She gasps when I nudge her thighs apart. I feel for the raised marks at the crease of her thighs. Her lips form a rounded O.

"What do I taste like?" she asks.

My grin is slow. "Warm honey mixed with cinnamon."

"Really?" Her eyes are bright as she preens. "You tasted spicy."

I chuckle at her description. I've never shared my blood with anyone. And I never will. All that I am is for this woman.

"Do you need any more?" she asks.

"I need all of you," I say as I take her lips.

"Are you going to turn me?"

"No. Never. I told you, I will spend the rest of my life with you. When your life is over, I'm coming with you."

"What if I want to be like you?" she asks.

I pull away from her, my face hardens. "You don't. I won't. I won't turn you into a monster."

Her hand comes to my cheek. "You're not a monster."

I close my eyes and turn my face into her hand. I

do not want to have this conversation anymore. Thankfully, she seems to sense that and changes the subject.

She scoots away from me and heads towards the door leading to her closets. Her walk is sure, like she owns the place. Good. I want her to feel at home here since this is where she will reside from now on.

"Can you look at pictures and paintings of the sun?" she asks.

"Yes, of course."

She feels on the wall and finds the light switch. The closet fills with fluorescence. But she is my sun. Like a moth to a flame, I follow her.

"I'll take a picture when I'm out today," she says. "The sunset over the Durand vineyard is the most beautiful. I want you to see it."

"Out?"

"I have to meet my brother and sister to sign some paperwork."

My first response is *the hell you will*. But I've matured, evolved. "I'll come with you."

"The meeting is at five. The sun won't be down yet. And you don't have to come."

She slips on another sundress, white this time. All of her wounds are healed. Her skin is perfect against the color of innocence, an innocence that I've claimed as my own.

"Tell them to change the time," I say.

Her back straightens as she buttons up the dress. But not in the sexy way of a submissive who has been put in her place. It's in the way of a fierce woman who has her hackles up. I brace myself for a fight that she will lose. But her gaze softens and her hand cups my chin. Now I am putty in her hands.

"This is about last night," she says. "The accident?"

How can I tell her it's about her whole life and that I need her to spend every moment of it with me as her protector, her pleasurer?

"It's just down the road. There isn't much traffic. If it'll make you feel better, I'll call my brother to pick me up. He's an excellent driver. He's never had so much as a fender bender."

"The hell you will," I growl. "Over my dead body will he come near you."

Her hand jerks away as if I'd burned her. "You still think he's tried to hurt me? Hadrian, that's ridiculous. Arneis loves me. He helped raise me."

"He's behind the raid of the club. And then we find ourselves run off the road and wrapped around a tree not long after."

"That was an accident."

She steps around me and heads back for the bedroom. The fire is dying. Carignan disappears into the darkness. But I see her just fine.

"Accidents and mishaps follow you. You're not leaving my sight."

"You don't own me, Hadrian," she says as she steps into a pair of flats.

"Perhaps you forgot our earlier conversation. You are mine."

"Sure." She comes to stand toe to toe with me. "Here in the bedroom. It's sexy here. It's not cute in any other room. And I'm leaving this room."

She takes a step to the door that leads out into the backyard, but I am on her in less than a second. She balls her hands into fists and puffs out her cheeks. It would be adorable under different circumstances.

"Hadrian, move out of my way."

"No. I can't."

Her entire body deflates. Her cheeks hollow. Her fingers hang limp at her sides. "Don't make me choose between you and my family."

The stake is back at the crash site. Yet somehow it pierces my chest all the way through. Why was I never enough? Domitia had always needed other lovers. And now Cari wants to run to her family instead of staying with me.

"I love you," she says. Her tone is a plea. It feels like a knife twisting in my heart.

Yes, this is familiar. The pain of love. The sharp needles in my chest. The inability to take a full breath.

"But you can't hold me captive."

If you live long enough, history will repeat itself. Cari's words are Domitia's last words to me down to the last syllable.

There was nothing I could do to hold onto Domitia. She made the decision to walk into the sun.

Cari doesn't go to the exit that leads to the hall. She goes to the exit from the first time she came into this room. The one that leads outside to the sun.

"Step back," she says.

I stand still. I can't move. My limbs no longer work. My heart stops beating.

"Hadrian, I don't want to hurt you."

She can't hurt me. Not when she's killed me. She's chosen others over me. Her hand on the door knob confirms it.

"I'll call you later and we'll talk."

She pulls the door open, but only a fraction. The sun is low, nearly swallowed up by the mountains.

Still, a soft ray of sunlight breaks into the darkness breaching my safe place. Cari steps through the crack of the door. I am powerless to stop her. For the second time in my life, I watch as the woman I love walks into the rays.

30

———

Cari

I'm not sure if I'm happy or disappointed that Hadrian doesn't follow me out of the bedroom. I suppose he can't since the setting sun shines its muted light on my face.

But he doesn't shout after me either. He doesn't call my name. He doesn't move.

Part of me is worried I really hurt him by leaving. But this is not how I am going to live my life. He can own my heart, he can be the master of my body, but he can't control me. I've finally taken the reins of my life back from fate and I'm captaining this ship. He'll have to get used to that.

We can talk it out later tonight when I'm done with family business. Because that's what I do now. I talk my problems out instead of jumping out of an airplane to deal with them.

See, grown.

I'm standing at the end of the drive when Arneis pulls up less than ten minutes after I call him. He does not look pleased as I climb into the passenger seat of his sensible town car. I pull the seatbelt strap over my torso and buckle up like a responsible adult.

See, grown.

"Really, Cari?" Arneis starts right in. For most of my life, he hasn't had to pull the big brother-bad cop card. Because I've been a saint.

Up until last year.

But my brother isn't tugging me out of a club at four in the morning... because he missed me at Club Toxic. Well, he's not tugging me out of a plane or scooping me from a lifeboat in the middle of the ocean. I'm just leaving my boyfriend's house after a night of passion... and a couple of near death experiences.

"How long have you known this guy?"

"Two?" I rewind the clock in my head. "No, three days."

"You were raised better than this, to sleep around with a man, and a man like that."

My foot presses into the floor of the car, as if I can hit the brakes. "A man like what, Arneis?"

Arneis purses his lips, like he's trying to hold something in. But he's never been good at keeping secrets or keeping silent. "Do you know the type of people he's associated with? The lowest of creatures."

"Like Lucius Frangelico at Club Toxic?"

Arneis' jaw tenses. I can hear him grinding his molars. His fingers are white as they grip the steering wheel. His lips purse once more, but this time he holds his tongue.

"Did you have anything to do with the raid last night?" I ask.

"What do you know about that?"

I try to swallow the lump in my throat before I go on. But the obstruction is cold, thick, and somehow it burns.

"I was there," I manage to say. "It was you, wasn't it?"

Oh god. Could Hadrian have been right? Could my brother be trying to kill me?

"You don't understand," says Arneis.

He pulls over to the side of the road. The sun has nearly set. In just a few moments it will be dark.

My world is upside down as I look at my big brother. Arneis taught me to ride a bike. He drove me and my friends to the mall in middle school. He came to every one of my high school soccer games even though I sat on the bench for over half of the games.

"There were a lot of debts with the vineyard. Dad owed people, not all of them nice. I've been doing my best to pay for things so you and Mare wouldn't know. The only way to keep it all going was to start the political bribes again. I didn't want to. But I had no choice until we sold the vineyard. Then I'd be able to clear all the debt."

My brain is so preoccupied with redrawing the past with my brother as a villain that I don't hear the words that exonerate him. It takes me a moment to replay his confession. When I do, I see that there is a threat. But it's not to me.

"So you extorted people like Frangelico?" I ask.

Shame shines through Arneis' eyes. It's easy to identify because I know it so well.

Here I thought I was the only one suffering after Papa's death. But Mare was struggling alone in the vineyard. And now I learn Arneis has been struggling over the books. Meanwhile, I've been playing fast and loose with my life.

"I never thought I'd be that kind of politician, that kind of man. But these are bad people. I'm not going to seek reelection, if this is what I have to do. I'll come back to the vineyard. We'll make it work. Papa would've wanted it that way."

I sigh. I didn't realize I've been holding my breath. "You had nothing to do with the failed parachute or the cut harness or last night's accident."

"What are you talking about?" He looks me over. "You were in an accident?"

"I'm fine. Everything's fine. Could you drive me back to Hadrian's? I just need to tell him something real quick."

Arneis glances at his watch. "We'll be late and..."

I don't hear anything else he says. A dark figure appears in front of the car out of nowhere. It's a woman. She has the palest skin and whitest hair. Her whiteness is stark in the dusk of night. She smiles and that's when I see the fangs.

31

Hadrian

The invaders have retreated beyond the horizon. I remain holed up inside. My boundaries have been breached. My defenses are down. The scene inside the walls of what was once my safe haven is that of a massacre as the white sheet from the bed slips onto the floor; a sign of surrender.

Darkness steals into the room. Not the dark of night. This is an empty darkness, devoid of moonlight, devoid of any essence. I know then that I must still retain my soul because my entire being feels plunged into a murky depth.

Cari is gone and I am hollow. A shell.

This is nothing like what I felt when Domitia died. That devastation was a stroll on a deserted highway. This feels as though I've been tossed over and into a raging sea during a hurricane.

I lost the power in my legs long ago. My bare ass sits on the cold floor. My head hangs down. My gaze remains fastened to my empty hands.

But only for a second.

Suddenly my hands are filled with wood and plaster. Blood trickles from my nail beds down my wrists. I look up to see that the wall in my bedroom now has a gaping hole in it, one the size of the hollow space in my chest now that she is gone.

I'm not sure when, but soon I'm no longer alone. The company to my misery is not welcome. I neither say nor do anything to usher it away.

"I heard doors opening before dusk settled," says Gaius. He is sitting beside me. Where his legs are covered in fine silk, mine are bare. His hands are clasped together in his lap, as though he plans to sit for a long while. "For a moment I assumed it was you on your daily rampage with the morning star. But with the new love in your life, I doubted you were still facing off against the sun."

I don't answer. I stare into the darkness. I can see everything, but I focus on nothing.

"She didn't slam doors as she left," Gaius continues. "Normally I would take that as a good sign when a woman leaves my bed. But then I come to find you here, butt ass naked on the floor, sitting in front of your patio door."

I lift my head, but not to look at Gaius. I bang it once, twice, three times against the wall. When I let my head come to rest there is a hole in the wall that cradles me.

Gaius nods his head as though that is my answer to the question he still hasn't asked. He still doesn't ask. He continues to deduce.

"For the brief moment that I met her, Cari didn't seem to me the theatrical sort. I didn't get the impression that she was emotionally abusive and would manipulate you like Domitia."

"Manipulate me?" I turn my head to face Gaius.

The male's robe is open and his chest is revealed. Over his left pec is an embroidered cross with a sword and a reef; a symbol of the Spanish Inquisition. I have the same marking, as does Viri. We are three males who have been dealt more than our fair share of misery in this world. No matter how much we try to turn our lives around and move away from pain, it always seems to follow us.

"Domitia slammed doors," says Gaius. "She broke furniture and dishes when you didn't give her her way. And sometimes even when you did. She liked the drama. She reveled in the pain. Your pain especially, because you were her shining knight."

Now I turn my body to face my friend. There was never any love between Domitia and Gaius. She liked his cock. He was her sired. Behind closed doors, Gaius always made it plain to me that there were no tender feelings for the woman I loved. Only devotion and gratitude for the new life she'd given him. But he never disparaged her.

He encouraged me to move on over the centuries. To find someone new. But he never spoke ill of the love she and I shared.

"Domitia needed to keep poking at you to get what she needed. Harder and harder each time. That's why she always came back to you, you know. You gave her what she needed most." He looks me square in the eye as he drops a grenade on my vision on the past. "Misery."

"Domitia loved me," I insist. But my pronouncement isn't as vehement as it would've been a few days ago.

"I don't doubt that. But it was a sick kind of love, Hadrian. Surely, you can see that now. She'd break your heart and disappear for years. I swear you are the first case of Stockholm Syndrome."

I turn back to the door where Carignan left me. I don't want to hear any more about Domitia. Her pale skin and white-blonde hair are a distant memory. What's in its place now is Carignan's sun-kissed skin and spirited gaze. I won't be forgetting her face anytime soon.

"Sometimes I feel a cold breeze and I wonder if she's still here," says Gaius. "But that's impossible. You saw her walk into the sun."

It's Carignan's body I see walk into the sun now. Only she didn't scream as the rays touched her. She didn't disappear as soon as she walked out.

"You did see her go?"

I turn and glare at Gaius. "You see that I am down, on the ground, on my ass. And you're going to kick me?"

Gaius flattens his lips. "What happened between you two?"

"We argued and she walked into the sun."

"Are we talking about you and Domitia? Or you and Cari?"

I bang my head against the wall again, but the

impact isn't the same now that there's a hole there. Plaster crumbles down around my shoulders.

"You need to go after Carignan," says Gaius.

"She left." I motion to the closed door.

"But she didn't slam the door. Cari's human. She can walk into the sun without burning to a crisp. The sun is down now. What are you waiting for?"

"She didn't choose me." My empty hands ball into fists. I bang them against my legs. "She wants to be with others."

"There's another man?" Gaius runs a hand through his hair and then tugs at his lower lip. "She didn't seem like the type. But I guess you never know to look at them. And they say it's always the good girls you need to watch out for."

"No, not another man. Her family; her brother and her sister."

Gaius opens his mouth. Then closes it. Then tries again. "She went home to her family and you're having a meltdown?"

My patience has gone. Gaius can see it in my eyes because he holds up his hands as though to ward off an impending attack.

"Hadrian, they're her family. You don't need to compete with them. The love of a family is different than the love between a man and a woman. I can't believe we're having this conversation. There needs to be a vampire birds and bees talk."

"I told her not to go," I insist.

"What if she told you to choose between her and us?"

"I don't understand the question."

"Wow. Okay. Kick in the nuts for the bromance. But you can have Carignan, and her family, and your family too. You bring us all together to be one big happy, dysfunctional family."

Maybe. Could I have overreacted? She did say she would call me later, and she's never gone back on her word in the three days that I've known her.

But there's still my suspicions of her brother. Cari was so sure Arneis would never hurt her, but I've seen too many humans turn on one another to not be cautious.

"Are we having an orgy?" Viri stands in the door in a pair of swim trunks and combat boots. He holds a blood bag in one hand and a phone in the other.

"You missed it," says Gaius. "We're done."

"So, Carignan's the type to like the double-tap?"

I sigh, but I'm too weary to correct Viri. Gaius snorts his laughter. Viri does not sound excited about the prospect.

Like me, Viri isn't fond of sharing women. Not

even when Domitia liked to share him with other women. She'd always brag about the size of Viri's member. Donkey Man, she used to call him and put him on display for other females. Sometimes she put his wares on sale when she needed cash quick.

"You what?" The shrill voice comes from the phone in Viri's hand. "What have you done with my sister? I will call the cops. I will call the FBI."

Viri holds the phone out in front of him. The screeching voice amplifies, as do the threats. "Someone called Mary is on the telephone for Carignan."

I scramble to my feet and grab the phone from Viri. "Marechal," I say calmly into the phone. "That was a misunderstanding."

"Just guys being guys," Gaius offers unhelpfully.

"I defended you to Arneis," Marechal is shouting. "He told me you were bad. And now-"

"No one has touched Cari but me," I say. "No one ever will. You can ask her yourself."

And then Marechal says the only thing that scares me more than the sun.

"She's not here. She's more than an hour late. So is Arneis. Neither of them are answering their phones."

32

Cari

I am bound. My hands are tied behind my back. The ropes bite into my flesh, coming away with pieces of my skin. The metallic smell of my blood is in the air.

I open my eyes but all is dark, save a sliver of light. No, not light. It shimmers in a way that light cannot.

The shimmer comes closer. It moves like waves, but it's not liquid. It's hair.

My mind reels back. The car. The woman on the road. Her pale skin and even paler hair. That's her.

"Who are you?" I ask.

"Don't act as though he hasn't talked about me," she says. Her voice is heavily accented. Spanish? No, she doesn't roll her R's. She barely sounds out her consonants. The English language on her tongue sounds clunky, untried, like she's come out of the Dark Ages and this is the first time she's ever spoken it.

I try to focus on what she's saying to me. She thinks I've been talking about her with somebody. "Who?"

My face is slammed to the side. The force is so strong, my whole body tries to turn. But my torso doesn't get far because of the binds.

I have experienced whiplash many times in my life. From braking hard and sudden in a speeding car. To the jerk and pull of the harness when I jump out of a plane. But I have never once in my life been slapped.

Long after the shock of the deed processes through my brain, long after the distress of the pain along my cheek, nose, and chin subsides, the ringing continues in my ear. The roaring echo acts like a silencer, or one of those sound canceling headphones that plays white noise while others around chat away. But it's like someone turns the volume down on the ringing in my ear because the shouting in the cafe breaks through.

"You are a home-wrecker," the white-haired woman screams at me. "Do you know what they did to whores like you in my time, women who lay with another's husband?"

Home wrecker? Husband? Her time?

It's hard for my brain to process what's happening. Too many new experiences are happening to me. I've been kidnapped, for real this time. I've been bound, and not in the good way. I've been assaulted physically, and now verbally.

"Well, nothing would happen to the man," she says in her heavy accent, which is hard to make out as she babbles. "But did you know the authorities would allow a husband who believed he was wronged to kill his wife?"

Wherever this chick is from, they are a backward culture. I'm hoping, wishing, and praying that she goes back there now and leaves me alone. I haven't touched her husband. I have only been with one man in my life.

The prickles of awareness start up my spine. Impossibility is dawning on me, along with her identity.

"Since he thinks I'm already dead, I suppose there is no problem with me killing you."

My entire body goes numb at her threat. Because I don't think it's a threat. I'm certain it's a promise.

"Domitia," I say. "You're Domitia."

When I was a girl, I got nightmares after watching *The Grinch Who Stole Christmas*. There's a scene in that movie when the Grinch is hatching his plan to steal all the presents from Whoville. As his heartless idea comes into focus, he smiles. The smile stretches across his face, all the way up to his eyes. His eyes squint upwards, along with his brows. And his ears curl into what look like horns. To this day the memory of the Grinch smiling makes me shudder.

That's how Domitia looks at me now.

"So he has spoken of me to you," she says through her grinchy grin.

Before I can answer, the room is flooded with lights. The bright light blinds me and I blink to adjust my vision. When I open my eyes again, Domitia is no longer there.

A second later I know that I'm wrong. She makes her presence known when I feel the binds pull.

The skin where I am cuffed tears. My joints

protest and then give in. At the first pop of bone from joint, I scream.

Hadrian said she liked to see people in pain. He also said she was dead. Maybe I'm dead? Maybe I'm in hell and this is my punishment?

"I was so certain he loved me so much that he'd walk into the sun for me. But he didn't," Domitia says as she rounds me. "I was very close to forgiving him when you ruined it all."

I know I should lift my head, to see where my enemy is. But I can't. The pain is too much. Terror fills me when I realize she's just getting started.

"He's been in such pain," she says. "Such perfect agony for centuries."

Even through my whimpering, I make out the madness in her voice. She says the words as though they bring her ecstasy. Like she is getting high off of simply knowing that Hadrian was suffering.

This bitch is crazy. How had Hadrian ever loved her?

"Decades upon decades of shame and guilt, all my hard work, now all gone because of you."

"You say you love him? That's not love. Pain is not love."

Domitia laughs. The sound hurts my ears. But not as much as the cane she takes to my back.

I can't bow my back to relieve any of the agony. The small inch that I move to absorb her strike sends even more pain through my dislocated bones.

"You childish human. You have no idea what love is. You have no idea what pain is. You play with your life, falling from the sky, walking up in the sky. You want to die."

The sick realization grasps hold of me. "You, you cut my harness. You ran us off the road last night."

"Of course I did." Domitia digs her nails into my scalp and wrenches my hair back. Her eyes are lifeless. Her fangs glisten in the overhead lights. "Is no one paying attention to me?"

"But Hadrian," I say. "Hadrian was in that car. He nearly died."

She tsks, making an annoyed sound, and then shoves my head down. "He's immortal, you imbecile."

"He was nearly staked alive."

She brushes the notion away with her hand. "I would stake him for fun all the time when we were together. And we will be together again. Your death will crush him, and then he'll come back into my arms, more miserable than when I left him."

My death? I feel the adrenaline rush through me.

But I am not up high ready to jump. I am not bound by Hadrian awaiting the pleasure he brings.

This is a harness I can not get out of. This is a plane that's not going my way. This is a plank walk that I will fall from.

"You're going to feel a lot of pain before I'm done," Domitia says, her voice pleasant in its promise. "You'll beg for death. I guarantee it."

33

———

Hadrian

I inhale the night's air. The wind is punctuated with the smell of ripe grapes, chemicals, and manure. I ignore them all and focus on the singular scent that has turned my world right-side up.

The smell of Cari is strong in my nose. The taste of her is still on my lips. The only thing missing is the actual feel of her in my hands.

Letting her walk out that door earlier this evening was the biggest mistake of my life. Not because I thought she was walking into danger. Because I was too wrapped up in my past pain to hear what she was saying to me. What she was asking of me.

She wasn't trying to leave me. I understand that now.

I'm going to make a lot more mistakes in this relationship. It's inevitable, since my only prior relationship was with a homicidal maniac. There's going to be a lot of deprogramming in my future. But I need to find Cari first.

There's still the possibility that Arneis is trying to kill her. But that possibility grows smaller with each passing moment.

Gaius is on the phone with Frangelico now. The vampire king tells us that Arneis was behind the raid last night. But the night before that, when Carignan was on her plank walk in the sky, Arneis had been in another meeting with Frangelico's human business partners all day. He couldn't have learned about the plank walk in time to sabotage it.

After I'm able to talk Marechal down from calling in the US Army to my home, she tells us that the night before, the night that Cari fell from the sky and into my arms, Marechal and Arneis were at home all day. They'd been arguing over the future of the vineyard while Cari was MIA. So once again, neither of them knew what Cari was up to, or had the time to interfere with her plans.

But I know that strap was cut before she was in the sky. I know there was no other vehicle last night, just a bright light. And now she and her brother are missing. When I find who's behind this, I will take them back to the dungeons of Spain and show them what I am truly capable of.

Gaius and I follow Cari's scent down the lane from our house. She didn't get far. Her essence is still in the air.

It doesn't matter where her captor took her, I will find her. I will track them down. Then I will torture him slowly, over days, over years. Bringing him back to life just so I can take his life even more slowly.

How could I have let her walk out this morning? After promising I'd go into the sun for her.

Just as I did with Domitia.

I've lived long enough that I should learn from my past. But I suppose I didn't learn any valuable lessons when I was with Domitia. I let her turn me inside out and call it love.

Cari crawled inside my barren heart cavity and became my heartbeat. The only pain I feel is the emptiness of not having her safe in my arms.

Carignan taught me what love truly is. Or rather, I'm learning through her.

Love is actually caring about what the person thinks and feels. I'm not good at that outside of the bedroom. But I'll work hard to improve.

Love is putting someone else's happiness before my own. Again, another failing grade when I step outside the bedroom. But I'm willing to practice until perfection.

Love is trusting that when someone walks away it doesn't mean they're gone forever. This will be my hardest lesson. But I'll begin my mastery as soon as I have Carignan back in my arms.

I will find her. I will save her. And then I will shower her with my love.

Cari's scent grows stronger as we get further down the lane. In the distance, I spot a town car. The license plate is a government issue. Could that be Arneis' car?

It must be. I remember she called him for a ride. I can't see her, but I can smell her sweet scent in the air.

My pulse races as I speed up. Then I nearly trip over my feet with my next inhale. There's also the smell of blood in the air. Her blood.

The car is stopped on the side of the road. It is not damaged. There was no crash.

I push myself faster until I am at the car. There is a body slumped over in the front seat. I see a dark head and know that I am alive because my heart stops. The blood, her blood, that is in my veins goes cold.

But it isn't her.

It's a man. It's her brother. Arneis is alive, but only barely. Blood is coming from his neck. Then I see it; puncture wounds.

A vampire attack.

But who?

"Do you smell that?"

Gaius' voice sounds strange. It's tinged with fear. It's strange because Gaius is never afraid.

I inhale again. Then I smell it, too. Instead of desire, instead of passion, true terror crawls up my spine.

"Tell me I'm imagining this Hadrian," Gaius says. "Tell me it can't be her."

Shifters aren't the only paranormals who know scent. Vampires have enhanced senses of smell as well. There are smells you never forget. The smell of your mother. The smell of your favorite dish. The smell of your maker.

Domitia. The scent of her is clear, unmistakable, alive.

Her scent intermingles with Cari's. It's all over Arneis. The car is where Cari's scent ends.

Wherever they went they didn't walk. Or perhaps she blurred. Trying to follow the scent of a vampire moving at top speed is near impossible.

"How?" demands Gaius. "How could this be?"

"I don't know." My voice is barely a whisper.

"You said she walked into the sun."

"She did. I saw her."

"Are you sure? You saw her burn?"

No. I didn't see her burn. She stepped out. She screamed. And then she was gone.

I turned away. I didn't want to go. She told me if I loved her I'd walk into the sun with her. But I hesitated. And I've paid for my hesitation with guilt and shame for hundreds of years. Until...

"It's exactly the long, suffering game she loves to play with you."

She wouldn't. I don't say that out loud. It sounds juvenile just in my head.

She would. She did. Here was her scent on the side of my vineyard. My new love, my true love, Cari is gone. And I stand in more pain than I've ever withstood in my long life.

Inside the car, Arneis is coming to. His wounds are significant, but he'll live. I need him conscious now, so I take my wrist between my teeth and tear. I wrench his head back and force my blood into his mouth.

"Where is Cari?"

The man stares into my eyes. His brown gaze is so like his sister's. "A ghost. A white-haired ghost."

There's no more denying it. It's true. Domitia is alive and she has Cari.

"Where would she be?" Gaius asks me. "Where would she take her?"

"Somewhere I'll find them. She'll want me to see."

34

———

Cari

Pain.

All I feel is pain. Pain in every part of my body. Pain even outside of my body. It's in the air molecules pressing against my skin. It's in every inhale. It's in the dust mites that touch my lips, my fingertips, my hair.

I've stopped blinking and just keep my eyes closed. I can't stop twitching, the pain in my extremities won't let up. I want to stop breathing. I want to stop existing if that means the pain will end. But the moments stretch on.

Most of the time, the pain is constant. Like a flat

line at the top of a mountain. And then it increases, taking me higher to a peak I never want to reach. But at the same time, I do want to reach it. Thinking that if I can just get past the next level, I can survive it.

Each time I reach the next summit, I am even more wrong than the last time. The pain spikes unbearably higher. The new flat line takes even longer to level out. At some point it never does.

There was a time I liked heights. A time I liked the adrenaline. But there is so much adrenaline in my blood right now I'm sure I'm bleeding it out. All that I want now is to be drained dry. No more fight. No more flight. Just an end.

But it won't end.

Sharp teeth puncture my neck. They puncture my arms. They puncture my lower calves.

"You do taste sweet, I'll admit."

The vampire bite is not the orgasm Hadrian said it would be. There is a spark of pleasure at the first prick, but Domitia likes to chew her food.

It hurts.

Everything hurts.

Why is she hurting me?

"You are going to help me make him miserable," she says. Still in that thickly accented, pleasant tone.

As if we were girlfriends talking about our Saturday night dates.

I know she's talking about Hadrian. I don't want to make Hadrian miserable. I want to make him happy. I love him.

I must say this out loud though I don't hear myself say it. There is only ringing in my ears. Ringing and her terrible voice.

"Love is pain," she shouts.

I wince, but that hurts. I try to shake my head, but the effort hurts. Even if I could, I know it won't accomplish anything.

"Happiness is a mirage. It never lasts. The only thing in life that does last is pain. You are brought into this world causing your mother pain. You are disappointed every day and sleep in pain. Pain is the truth."

No. What she's saying is a lie. I can see that much through all this pain she is inflicting.

Hadrian made me feel good. When he came into my life he brought pleasure. When I fell asleep in his arms I felt safe. His love, and my love for him, is the only truth I am certain of.

"You were trying to give my Hadrian a lie. But now I'm back. I'll take care of his heart and make him miserable again."

He isn't her Hadrian. He is my Hadrian. I want to fight for him. I need to fight for him. I need to fight for our love.

But how, when I hurt so much? How, when I am bound by this mad woman? How, when all I want to do is skip to the end I know she has planned for me?

I don't want to die. I want to live. I want to live with Hadrian. I need to live for him. I can't let her win.

There is another impact on my body. I'm not sure where. I'm not sure with what. The pain is instant and it radiates everywhere.

I think I scream. But I'm not sure. My ears still ring. My throat is so dry I feel like I've swallowed nails. All the pain she's delivered to me welcomes this next bout of pain. All the prickles and stings and bites are making friends. They're settling in to stay on my torn skin, inside the cracks of my bones. Great, come on in.

Domitia doesn't strike me again for a while. The pain rages on, but I reach a plateau. Breathing isn't entirely impossible in this tiny sliver of relief. Blinking still won't be possible, so I leave my eyes closed.

I know that we are moving. I feel the wind on my face. I smell the air, earth, berries.

I know the smell of these berries. They are old, and yet new. Berries from a far away land that are freshly planted in the Arizona soil. We are back at the vineyard. We are back at Hadrian's vineyard.

No. I have to fight. I have to warn him. I have to get away.

But I can't move a single limb. It feels as though everything in me is broken. Everything but my will and my heart.

I will not give in to her. I will not let her win.

My brain makes out a knocking sound. Followed by a gasp. It's a masculine gasp. I've never heard a man gasp in terror before.

"Let me in, Viri, darling."

"No." Viri's voice is a low whine, like a wounded animal.

"Let. Me. In." Domitia punctuates every word. "Or you'll be punished."

There's another masculine whine. I crack open one eye and see Viri sink to his knees. The big man is near tears. His gaze is full of sorrow as he glances at me, and then down. He nods his head and we move across the threshold.

I close my eyes again. The next time I come conscious I am surrounded by Hadrian's scent. I am in his room. I am in his bed.

Domitia placed me here, in this place where I realized I wanted to experience my life more than I wanted to lose my life. She has placed me here to die.

I know that I will. But I'm going to hold on for as long as it takes to see Hadrian, to let him know that he gave me back my life. To let him know what we had was love and I wouldn't want to have lived my life without knowing him. That I would do it all again if it meant that I would have his love, even just for the short time that I have.

35

———

Hadrian

I tear at my hair, pulling clumps from the roots. I clench my hands into fists until my nails begin to crack and bleed. I throw back my head and let out a cry that silences all creatures of the night.

I cannot find her.

I have looked everywhere. Her home. The airfield where she took her dives. The two buildings where she took her walk across the sky. Her family's vineyard where I had to confront Marechal. Luckily, Gaius was able to divert Marechal's homicidal attentions against me by depositing her injured brother into her care.

I am at the very end of my rope. I don't know where else to look. But I know Cari lives. I feel her inside me.

She is the beat of my heart. She is the pulse in my veins. She is my breath, and the very fact that I am still breathing, I know that she is still on this plane of existence.

I hear a phone ringing. It's not mine. Mine has remained silent for the last few hours that I've been searching for my heart.

Gaius pulls a device from his pocket and answers. I can hear the conversation from the other end. It's just two words. But those two worlds rock my world.

"She's here."

Gaius doesn't ask Viri which she. In this case, we both know his statement is plural. They are both there. Domitia has taken Cari back to my home.

Why hadn't I thought of that first? I claim to know the madwoman so well. But after three days with Cari, I see that I don't know my former lover at all.

No, I retract that title as I blur across the vineyard. Domitia was never my lover. She was my seducer first. She murdered the innocent youth that I was. Then she jailed my mind and caged my heart.

I just didn't realize that she fed me on a daily diet of torture and not love.

Not five minutes later, I burst through the front door of my home to find Viri huddled in the corner. The cell phone is still in his ear. I realize now just how damaged she made my blood brother. How damaged she made us all.

Viri is too broken to believe he could be loved. Gaius, the only one of us who saw her clearly, is too jaded to ever consider love. Me? My vision, my mind is so twisted that I never knew what love was. But no longer.

"I called for help," says Viri.

"You did." I touch his shoulder briefly. "I'm here."

I leave him there. He'll survive. Cari needs all of my attention.

I follow Cari's scent to my bedroom. When I see her I nearly fall to my knees. My love, my heart, my soul, she is twisted as she lays on the bed.

Her body is bent. Her limbs hang loose. Her face is black and blue.

Murder is on my mind. Every torture technique I have ever learned springs into my vision. But I push it all aside when Cari opens her eyes and finds my gaze.

I am on her. I am with her. I would take her pain

if I could. Once again in less than twenty-four hours, I tear into my wrist and place my blood to her lips.

Her lips are cracked, broken, bleeding. She tries to open her mouth, but I can see that that even small motion pains her. Death will not be good enough for Domitia.

"Oh, this is all so touching. Like a sappy movie on that channel that does the silly holiday cards."

The voice is from my nightmares. I struggle with turning to face Domitia and staying with Cari. If Carignan doesn't make it, I need for my face to be the last thing that she sees. I need for my declaration of love to be the last thing she hears. I need for my kiss to be on her lips before she takes her last breath.

"She's going to die," says Domitia. "I made sure it'll be slow and painful so that we can both watch."

I whip around to her at those words. There she stands. She is as thin and pale as a wraith. She's dressed in black, which sets her porcelain skin in stark relief. Though she's in dark clothing I see the dark spots of Cari's blood all over her gown.

"I even popped corn," she says. "A wondrous invention for watching entertainment. Want some?"

Her thin fingers offer me a handful of the fluffy treat. "I'm going to kill you."

"Again?" She grins. "The pain, the shame of my

death kept you alive all this time. And you've made something of yourself. I keep Serrano wines in my cellar, truly delicious work. You three should be thanking me for all your success."

Thanking her?

"Though that's not the reason I did it," she continues. "I always intended to come back to you, darling. I always imagined the joy you'd feel after decades of thinking I was dead. All that pain bottled up for a big release." Her face transforms as her gaze finds Cari. "And she ruined it."

I place myself in Domitia's line of sight to block her view of Cari. Her gaze flicks back to me. I note, for the first time in hundreds of years, that her eyes are vacant black holes. How had I thought love shone through those void orbs?

"I burned for you," she says. She blinks and waggles her head, popcorn spills from her hands as she confesses. "Not to a crisp, obviously. I drank a witch's potion to step into the sun. It only lasted for a moment. I did get a touch crusty on the edges though. I was curious what the burn would feel like. It was quite rousing. I had one of my human slaves toss a cloak over me after I dropped from your sightline. It took me an entire week to heal."

I am lightheaded at her revelations. Not only did

she fake her death, but she's also been watching me all these years. Taking joy in my pain.

Gaius was right. It's not just her who's sick, I am a complete invalid. I never saw what a lie she was. Now I do. And I am also healed. The scales have fallen from my eyes and I see this creature for who and what she truly is.

"At first I was quite heartbroken that you didn't follow me out into the sun. But as I watched you burn on a daily basis for me, I knew that you truly loved me. It was so touching. I'd planned to come back to you a couple of months later, but when I saw how you grieved, it filled me with such love for you."

She says that four letter word and my stomach clenches. My chest hardens. My throat itches with bile.

"I loved watching you in pain over my death. But I always planned to come back to you. I've checked on you over the decades. Each time I saw that you still grieved it made me so aroused. But now we can be together again, at last."

Domitia tosses more popped corn in her mouth. Much of it falls to the floor. I note the red stains on her hands, Cari's blood.

My vision goes red. But for some reason, my

hands aren't on her neck. For some reason, I am not tearing her limb from limb.

"Hadrian," Cari whispers.

I turn away from Domitia. My heart flushes of its hatred of her the moment my back is to her. My mind is no longer on her. With the sight of my true love in my eyes, I am filled with nothing but love.

Carignan lifts her mangled hand. I am on my knees, helping her bring her fingers to my face. I kiss each of her bruised knuckles gently.

"You saved my life," says Cari.

"You saved mine," I say. "You showed me what love truly is."

"I did," she agrees. She tries to grin but instead grimaces in pain.

Anger and rage push against the love I feel for her. My fingers want to rip something, someone apart.

"Don't walk into the sun tomorrow," says Cari. "I want you to live for me. Will you do that?"

"No, he won't," says Domitia. "He'll live for me because I know what he needs to keep him alive. He needs the pain. He craves it. Don't you, darling? Right now, you feel the life coursing through your dead veins as you watch her die."

I don't turn to Domitia. At the moment, I feel

nothing for her. Not even hatred. She is no longer a factor. I keep my gaze trained on what's important.

Cari.

More than anything I am determined that she will not die. If I am going to live, then so will she.

A shadow moves in the dark hall. Domitia is too engrossed in the tragedy she's created to notice. I'm too preoccupied with love and my new life's mission to care.

I tear open my shirt. I slice my nails through my chest. On the left side where my heart beats.

I lift Cari's head to my chest. She is unresponsive now. Still, I coax her to drink from me, to take everything I have in my heart.

From behind me, I hear Domitia gasp. There's not much that's ever frightened a woman who gets off on pain. Except the possibility of losing some of her power.

"Hello, dear," says Frangelico in his smooth, unhurried voice.

"Oh, Lucius, darling," Domitia's voice is wobbly with false certainty. "What a pleasant surprise."

"I got a call from your Virius," says Frangelico. "He told me you were in town."

"Really? I'll need to have a talk with my little Donkey Man."

"Let's you and I chat first. You are in my territory, after all."

The sounds of battle that rage behind me do not sound pleasant. I ignore it as I focus all of my attention on Cari and getting her to drink. I would hate to defy her last wishes, but I will. If she doesn't wake a vampire in the morning, then I will face the sun.

36

———

Cari

At least death is warm. I expected it to be cold with no blood running through my veins any longer. But my fingers aren't numb. My legs are stiff. I feel... good.

Well, my body feels good. It's my heart that's broken. I can't open my eyes, not when I know that I will never see Hadrian again.

I wonder if the warmth and toastiness I'm feeling is because I've landed in Hell. That wouldn't be fair since I didn't cause my death. I was murdered. I figure I should get a pass. Then I can see my parents.

But I note that the temperature of the room isn't warm. It's comfortable. It's just my skin that's snug.

No, wait. That's not my skin. It feels more like a blanket. Like a warm comforter stretched along my body and tucked in at the edges.

Hunh? Maybe this is heaven. I'm sure the devil wouldn't take this type of care of one of his new inhabitants.

If this is heaven, the air quality is pretty poor. I try to inhale. But I can barely take in a breath.

My lungs aren't working correctly. No, they don't seem to be working at all. I can breathe, but the air coming into my body feels hollow. Almost unnecessary.

My stomach feels empty and I have no urge to fill it. Almost as if I don't have need of food any longer.

Lying down feels good. But I'm not tired. Definitely not sleepy. I feel like I could run a mile. And for some reason I'm sure I could do it in less than a minute.

I hear a voice call my name. Immediately, I grimace. I know it's Hadrian. So why am I mad?

I told him not to follow me in death. But did I really expect him to listen? He is so determined to be the boss of me. I suppose now I have to let him be. I have no idea what to do in death. I just hope we can still have sex.

"Carignan."

His voice is soft, like a whispered prayer. Any irritation I felt melts away. I know it's sick, but I'm happy he followed me to the other side. A famous man once said that death could not part true love. That all it could do was delay it for a little while.

Hadrian didn't waste a moment to be with me in the next life. It's romantic. It's not stalking at all.

I turn my head to the sound of my name. It's not Hadrian that I see. It's not his deep voice. It's deep, but there is no accent.

"Carignan," the man says again.

He's tall with gray hair. He has a big, barrel chest and a smile that makes me feel like a kid on Christmas morning.

"Papa?"

My dad is standing in front of me. There is light around him. He is whole, and healed, and healthy. He's not bleeding. His eyes are open. So are his arms.

I run to him. I jump into his arms like I am a kid again. He folds me into his arms like I am still his little girl.

"Papa, I'm so sorry," I say. "I died. I didn't mean to this time. I tried to live. I fought so hard to live."

My father smiles down at me. He lifts his hand to my face. This time it reaches my cheek. I feel the soft brush of his fingertips below my eyes as he brushes a tear away.

Behind my father, I see a woman come into view. She has brown hair like mine, and brown eyes. It's been so long since I've seen her that it takes me a moment to recognize her.

"Maman?"

She doesn't touch me. She rests her head on my father's shoulder and simply smiles at me. The same love that warms me from my father's eyes shines from hers.

"Go," says my father. "Get out and live."

"What?"

It's the same words he said to me before he died. Why does he say them now when I am dead?

Before I can ask him, he slips from my grasp. He moves away from me, walking into the bright light with my mother on his arm. Even though they're retreating I can still feel them with me. In my heart.

"Carignan?"

This voice I know is Hadrian's. I turn around, but I don't see him. Just darkness. It's then I realize that my eyes are still closed.

I open them.

I see the dark, blackout blinds of Hadrian's room. The only light is the fire burning in the hearth. I'm lying down on his bed. All around me I smell the spicy scent of him. I can taste it on my tongue. I can feel it in my blood.

A memory flashes through my mind. It's of me and Hadrian. He has me locked in a tight embrace. My face is at his chest. My mouth is on his heart, taking in the blood directly from that organ.

I did die. But Hadrian didn't. He brought me back to life.

"There you are," he says as he brushes my hair away from my temple.

His touch before this moment always made me heated. It's an inferno now. My senses reach a height beyond 18,000 feet. I can feel the grooves of his fingerprints. I make out each of the unique lines that belong only to him. I can now tell his touch from anyone else's.

"Hey," I say.

"Hey."

"I'm not dead." It's all I can manage when so much is running through my head.

"That fact is debatable."

"I'm a vampire."

"I had to." His strong voice is a wary plea. "I had

to try and save your life. You made me want to live. I didn't want to do it without you."

The wariness invades his features. He's waiting for my reaction. Will I rage at him for turning me into what he is? Or will I thank him for bringing me back to him.

I sit up. I'm naked beneath the sheets. Perfect. It'll save time for what I have planned.

Hadrian ignores my naked chest. His gaze is still intent on my face, like he's still waiting for my reaction to what he's done, what he's turned me into.

"You brought me back to life," I say, "Back to you."

His eyes close. His sigh is heavy with relief.

I look down at my hands. The last thing I remember when I was awake was pain. Nothing but pain. And then his face. I clung to the sight of him until I couldn't hold my eyes open any longer.

"Where is she?" I ask. I don't want to speak her name. Luckily, I don't need to clarify.

"Gone."

"Gone-gone?" I ask.

He nods.

I don't ask for any elaboration. There's only one thing that I care about. "So your heart is all mine now."

I reach out to him, placing my hand over the tattoo on his heart, the one that marked him as the Prince of Pain. I want to etch over it with a mark of my own.

"I am all yours now. My body, my soul, and my heart."

"Yeah? *Sii uno ragazzo bravo*. Show me."

He grins at my words. He comes to his knees on the bed. He doesn't need to lord his power over me. He has my total devotion, my total submission, my total self.

Though I've been given this second life, I won't toy with it. I won't seek out danger. I won't taunt a true death.

I will protect my life. I will share it with this man who has given me a reason to live to the fullest. I will no longer harness myself and dangle the tether of my life.

Well... not unless Hadrian is holding the other end of the rope while I'm tied down to a bed.

"I want to take you to my cellar," he says.

"What's there?"

"My play room."

"You mean like video games or something?"

His grin is wicked. "Come see."

I follow him out of the house and down into the

earth. I'd follow him anywhere. When he opens the door to the dark dungeon of the cellar, I gasp. I don't step back. I step forward, ready to strap into whatever paces he wants to put me through.

I turn to him, offering him my wrists. "I'm yours."

"And I'm yours."

Hadrian spends the rest of the night, the rest of our forever, showing me that he is indeed the master at what he does. He is no longer the Prince of Pain. He has become my Prince of Pleasure.

Get ready for Gaius' story next in
Her Vampire Lord.
Turn the page for a sneak peek!

EXCERPT OF HER VAMPIRE LORD

Gaius

"Master Gaius, please may I suck your cock? "

My cock twitches in my pants, as though it will answer the woman's desperate plea. I'm only semi aroused. Most of my blood is still in my brain because my mind is elsewhere. That is why I came here in the first place; I need more blood in my system.

"I've been such a good girl, Master Gaius," says a different feminine voice from the first. "Please? Just the tip? I'll suck it so good, I promise."

I open my eyes and take a minute to focus. It's

dark in the private room. I don't need much light to see. My superior sight means I need only a pinprick for me to track my prey.

They are right where I left them, inside this locked room with leather padding for walls, chains dangling from the ceiling, and sex toys littering the floor. Both women are on the floor. Knees spread. Hands on thighs, bound together with fur-lined cuffs. Nipples tight, begging for attention. The dark buds remind me of the berries that should be growing in my vineyard and my mind wanders again.

For centuries, I have been able to grow grapes in any soil I dig my fingers into, be it the briny regions of France or the saline coasts of Spain. But here, in the dry desert of southwest America, my vines are refusing to yield.

"Please, Master Gaius, may I come?"

Once more, my attention is called back to the present. I focus fully on the two women on the floor. Their bodies are trembling, like an earthquake is waking beneath them, ready to break them apart. The earthquake is a pair of Sybian sex machines.

The two women sit astride the Sybians' saddles. Nestled between their thighs is a dildo with a ribbed base that vibrates against their clit at the front and their anus at the back. The controller is set to a low hum, just enough to tease but not send anyone into orgasmic spasms. Unless the rider has been astride for a long time.

Glancing at my watch, I realize I've been here for at least a half an hour, riding these women. The scent of their sex fills the room. The air is humid with their moist juices and sweat. Their areolas are bubblegum pink and Hershey brown from the pleasure. Their labia are more red than pink from the delectable abuse of the machine.

On their asses are dark marks from the flogger I used on them. The device sits at my feet now. Hershey Brown's gaze is fastened on the device as she pants her desire for more. Bubblegum Pink's eyes are closed, her head lolling back. On her neck are two twin pricks that have puckered another shade of pink; a tiny trail of red blood meanders down her long throat.

She tasted like a stick of gum after the flogging. Sweet at the first bite, but the flavor only lasted a few moments. I liked my food saccharine. Hence, the Sybians.

The girls should now be ripe for the taking. The endorphins should have flooded their blood by now, making for a satisfying two-course dinner. But I am an admitted food snob. I like my meals cooked perfectly.

I turn the dial from low to medium. The two women mewl. They're both on the cusp of coming. Hershey Brown's eyes flash golden, her inner animal eager to come out to play.

"I'll let the last one who comes suck my cock," I say.

Their purrs are guttural. I can see their pussies shiver at the thought, then shiver in earnest as I turn the dial up to high. Their mewls sound closer to the growls of wolves. I watch impassively, my fangs twitching more than my dick. I want them in my mouth, their endorphin-rich, sweet blood. Having me in their mouths?

I give an internal shrug.

Sex has always been a game for me. One that I could never afford to lose. If I didn't bring forth the pleasure for *her*, then there would only be pain for me.

The buzzing of the sex machines pulls me back to the matter at hand. The two pussy cats are shivering, and the dial has one more setting. Asshole that I am, I switch the dial past high and wait for them to erupt.

Their mewling fills my ears. The scent of their

juices fills my nostrils. The iron from their blood touches my tongue. But they hold out. I'm not sure if it's the competition between them or if they just really want to suck my cock. I don't really care so long as their hands stay bound. To have either of their claws on my flesh would bring back memories I have locked down tight.

I rise, waiting for the inevitable eruption. I think Bubblegum Pink will be the first to crash into orgasm. I loosen my belt buckle and take a step towards Hershey Brown.

A buzzing in my pants stops me. I look down at my phone. When I see the name on the caller ID, I immediately hit *talk*.

"Is she there?"

The caller doesn't even bother with hello. She has manners, I've seen them first hand. But she is a single-minded woman.

"No, Marechal," I say. "Your sister isn't here."

My brother Hadrian would never allow Carignan, his new eternal bride, to be unclothed before another. He has her locked inside his own private dungeon at our estates tonight, sating her more base needs in the privacy of our home.

"When do you expect her back?" asks Marechal.

This is the problem with turning new vampires.

Humans are so connected in this new world. People text, snap, chat, and DM constantly, not allowing anyone the ability to disappear. It would all be so simple if Marechal was made to simply forget about her sister. But Cari wouldn't hear of it.

Truth be told, I don't want to hear of it either. If Marechal were mind-wiped and made to forget her sister, she would have to forget me too. Though we've only had two encounters in person, I would sorely miss the disdain and dismissal in her gaze when she looks at me.

"I need to talk to her," says Marechal in her clipped, business voice. The woman is a logical, practical, methodical scientist through and through.

I haven't seen her make a single emotional move since I met her. She never has a hair out of place, not even when her sister went missing and her brother was in an accident. Marechal had taken a deep breath, begun a checklist of what to do, and assigned each of my brothers a task. I had wanted to snatch the pad and pen out of her hand, tug at the strands of her perfectly coiffed hair, and break the buttons of her starched shirt.

But I don't play with humans any longer. They're too fragile for my particular tastes. Plus, I never enjoyed wiping their minds when things got a little rough, which they always did with me.

"They'll be back from their honeymoon soon," I soothe, lying easily.

Hadrian likely has his bride bound to a Saint Andrew's Cross and is fucking the living daylights out of her. I can't very well tell her older sister that hunch. Nor can I invite her over to see that her sister is perfectly fine, because she isn't. Not yet.

Newly turned vampires are hungry beasts. It takes a while for them to gain control over their animal instincts. If Marechal happened upon Carignan during this adolescent stage of her new life, where she is completely uninhibited, indulgent, and self-centered, it would turn out bloody.

"Where are you?" Marechal asks. "It sounds like you're at an animal shelter filled with cats."

I turn back to the scene in one of Club Toxic's private sex dungeons. I'd nearly forgotten about the two pussies on the fucking machines. They are sweating profusely as they try not to come.

"I am," I say. "I'm at a benefit for wayward animals."

"You? I didn't take you for a philanthropist."

I'm not. "I give back." I don't.

I care only about my pleasure and the wellbeing

of my family. Carignan is now part of my family. She is my sister, and I will protect her as I do my brothers.

Hmm? Does that make Marechal my sister as well?

I don't like that thought. I'm more interested in what Marechal would look like if she were on one of the machines. Riding it without a stitch of fabric on her body. Her hair down and free. Her head thrown back as I slap her nipples until they are tight peaks.

"I'm going to get off now," Marechal says, and I nearly choke. "You'll call me the moment they walk in the door?"

Oh, she is still talking about her sister and Hadrian. "I give you my word."

"I'm still not entirely convinced this isn't a kidnapping, you know."

That is another thought I like: grabbing Marechal and absconding with her against her will. Modern women say they don't like that, but the billion-dollar romance novel industry begs to differ. Women like to be told what to do. I like to be the one telling them.

"You never told me when you wanted me to come over," she says.

"Come over?"

"To look at your vine."

I've had two dripping, mewling pussies at my feet all night. But at Marechal's words, my dick goes instantly hard.

"You said it's going through a rough patch?"

"There's nothing wrong with my vine."

"You said it had rot; you showed me, remember?"

Right. She's talking about the vineyard. My pristine grapes are having trouble in the acrid, dry Tucson soil.

"The Palmezzos had trouble with that soil too," Marechal goes on. "When I was a kid, the migrants who worked the land said that it was cursed."

I am a centuries-old vampire. I have seen more than my fair share of the unexplained, and lived long enough to learn the explanation. There is magic in the world, but there is no such thing as a—

"But you and I know there is no such thing as a curse," Marechal says. "I'm sure there's an explanation. I'll be over tomorrow."

"I'll come to you," I say.

"It would be much easier if I studied the vine in its native soil."

"Too dangerous. I mean, I wouldn't want to take you away from your business."

"I do have a busy day tomorrow."

"I'll come over at sundown."

"Fine," she says. "Just let me know when you hear from my sister. And do something about those cats."

And with that, she clicks off.

I turn my attention back to the dripping pussies. Hershey Brown's eyes are rolling back in her head. With a loud thud, she falls over. Bubblegum Pink grins in triumph. I guess I'll be fucking her mouth for the rest of the evening, though my dick has softened now that Marechal is no longer in my ear.

I reach for my belt again, but a second thud fills my ears. Bubblegum Pink has collapsed on the floor, her body shuddering from a toe-curling orgasm. When the tremors stop, both women lie in comatose heaps on the ground.

I'm not put out. I call one of the attendants to see to their aftercare. Then I pour myself a glass of wine. The color is a brown that shifts to a shade of purple in the low light. It is the exact color of Marechal Durand's eyes.

Start reading *Her Vampire Lord* now!

ABOUT INES JOHNSON

Lover of fairytales, folklore, and mythology, Ines Johnson spends her days reimagining the stories of old in a modern world. She writes books where damsels cause the distress, princesses wield swords, and moms save the world.

If you liked Ines' Vampires, then you'll love her Dragons; alpha male shifters, fated mates, and steamy romance with a touch of 80's nostalgia! To grab a free book from the world of the Last Dragons just visit https://ineswrites.com/ReaderGroup

MORE PARANORMAL ROMANCE BY INES JOHNSON

Dark Vintage
Her Vampire Prince
Her Vampire Lord
Her Vampire Knight
His Vampire Princess

The Last Dragons
The Dragon's Reluctant Sacrifice
The Dragon's Ambivalent Sacrifice
The Dragon's Willing Sacrifice
The Dragon's Rebellious Sacrifice
The Dragon's Compliant Sacrifice
The Dragon's Forbidden Sacrifice

The Moonkind Series
Moonlight
Moonrise
Moonfall

The Knights of Caerleon
First Knight
One Knight
Arabian Knight

www.ingramcontent.com/pod-product-compliance
Lightning Source LLC
Chambersburg PA
CBHW060906210726
48293CB00006B/1975